Sniff Bounces Back

It was Sniff, up and running but still fast asleep and thinking that someone had said 'Breakfast!' By the time he got his eyes properly open and saw Sal sticking out from under the bookcase, it was too late for him to put his brakes on. He tried doing an emergency stop by throwing his legs out sideways and crash-landing on his tum, but he must have hit a bit of that waxy paper you get on the inside of Mini Wheats boxes, because he did this really amazing wheelie, catching Sal with his backside and sending her spinning out from under the bookcase like a skittle in a bowling alley. I tried to jump out of the way and stubbed my toe on the hall table, Sal thumped her head, and Sniff finished up with his nose wedged under the bookcase.

Sniff Bounces Back

Ian Whybrow

Illustrated by
Toni Goffe

RED FOX

For the Steeles of Windfall House
Pat and Dave
Jason, Ben and Sal
And Sam and Jamie, my favourite Ghostbusters

A Red Fox Book

Published by Random Century Children's Books
20 Vauxhall Bridge Road, London SW1V 2SA
A division of the Random Century Group

London Melbourne Sydney Auckland
Johannesburg and agencies throughout the world

First published by The Bodley Head Children's Books 1990

Red Fox edition 1991
Text © Ian Whybrow 1990

Set in Plantin
Typeset by JH Graphics Ltd, Reading

Made and printed in Great Britain by
Cox & Wyman Ltd, Reading

ISBN 0 09 985540 2

Contents

Sniff and the Playgroup Gerbil

Sal was feeding Mini Wheats to the bookcase in the hall.

It was early Saturday morning – about half past six – and I was up, hoping to sort out a little bug in a computer program I'd got started on the night before. Dad had been helping me a bit and we'd been working in the sitting-room. The program was supposed to be a loop, but it kept freaking out when you'd gone about five steps. What I needed was a bit of peace so that I could concentrate. Peace with Sal around? Ha ha.

I thought that the best thing to do was to try sneaking past her while she was busy feeding the bookcase. It's weird, but she never seems to get tired of stuff like that. Last Sunday, after lunch, she tipped a load of apple pie and custard out of her bowl into the knife drawer. Dad said to her, 'Sal, that's not the rubbish bin!' and she said, 'He want some. He mouff open.' Makes you wonder what goes on in that little kiddie mind of hers. She and her friend Tom sometimes feed this tree in the garden by poking sucked Smarties into a hole in its trunk, and I've even seen Sal squeezing toothpaste down the loo and saying, 'Like it? . . . 'Snice, yum, yum.'

Anyway, here we were, Saturday morning, seven o'clock, me trying to sneak along the hall to the sitting-room and Sal lying flat on her tum, pushing Mini Wheats at the bookcase. The packet looked as if it had been opened by a pterodactyl, and bits of it were scattered around her. Just as well she hadn't got her hands on a packet of porridge or a squeezy bottle of tomato ketchup, or I'd have had to get Mum up to do something about it. As it was, I thought, well, nobody likes Mini Wheats that much anyway, so it was best to let her get on with it. I hitched up my pyjama trousers, took a deep, quiet breath and tiptoed sideways down the hall. I got right to the hall table without her looking up and I couldn't believe my luck when, just as I was reaching out for the sitting-room door-handle, she stuck her head right under the bookcase. Everything was going brilliantly until she started making clicking noises with her

8

tongue. I froze for a sec, wondering what the heck was going on and all of a sudden she bawled out, 'Here boy!'

That was it. BOY SCIENTIST'S DARING BID FOR PEACE FOILED BY CRAZED SISTER'S YELL. There was the loud screamy-scrape of the kitchen table being pushed aside at high speed, followed by the thump of a hairy head against the edge of the kitchen door and the KERRUCKA TADUCKER of clumsy great paws along the hall. It was Sniff, up and running but still fast asleep and thinking that someone had said 'Breakfast!' By the time he got his eyes properly open and saw Sal sticking out from under the bookcase, it was too late for him to put his brakes on. He tried doing an emergency stop by throwing his legs out sideways and crash-landing on his tum, but he must have hit a bit of that waxy paper you get on the inside of Mini Wheats boxes, because he did this really amazing wheelie, catching Sal with his backside and sending her spinning out from under the bookcase like a skittle in a bowling alley. I tried to jump out of the way and stubbed my toe on the hall table, Sal thumped her head, and Sniff finished up with his nose wedged under the bookcase.

I'm not quite sure who made most noise, because I was too busy hopping up and down going 'Ouch, ouch, ouch' and hanging on to my toe to think about the racket that Sal and Sniff were making at the same time. All I know is that by the time I'd cut down from 'Ouch' to 'Oooo', Mum and Dad had arrived. Dad had picked up Sal, and Mum was cuddling Sniff, and they were both picking their way barefoot among the prickly Mini Wheats, jigging their armfuls up and down and going 'There there, never mind.'

And did I get any there-theres? Sal was getting the back of her head rubbed, Sniff was getting his nose massaged, but the one person to suffer *mega*-damage had to look after his own toe. 'It'll probably go black,' I said, but nobody took any notice.

'What were you *doing* Sal?' Dad asked, 'What happened?'

'Miff eatin da gerby meckmus,' Sal said, pointing at Sniff who had got fed up with being cuddled, squirmed out of Mum's arms, and was now slurping and snapping among the Mini Wheats.

'What?' said Dad.

'Meckmus!' yelled Sal, hitting the top of Dad's head with her fist.

'Yes, I got that bit,' said Dad, who knew that 'meckmus' meant breakfast. 'But what's all this meckmus doing on the floor?'

'Nat da *GERBY* meckmus!' she screamed. She always screams when you can't understand what she's saying. She went stiff in Dad's arms and bent herself backwards as if she was going to do a backward dive on to the floor. Dad sort of scooped

10

her up before she did herself any damage and managed to wipe some nasty-looking gunge off her face with a hankie at the same time.

I was getting really cheesed off with this. 'Isn't anybody going to look at my toe?' I said. 'I think I need a splint or something.'

Mum didn't take any notice. She was squatting down, rubbing Sniff's nose, feeding him Mini Wheats and going, 'Poor old Snifty Wifta, he *did* bump his sad old nosy-wosy.' Dad put Sal down and she threw herself sideways on the floor, put her arm under the bookcase and started feeling about.

'What do you mean – "gerby meckmus"?' Dad asked her. When he got no answer, he turned to me. 'Ben, what's she talking about?'

'The playgroup gerbil. She means the gerbil. She's looking after it for the weekend and Dad, what about my toe? D'you reckon it needs an X-ray?'

'Then what the heck's it doing under the bookcase?' yelled Dad.

'Oh, my goodness!' said Mum, who until then had been concentrating on soothing Sniff, and she dropped on to her tum to have a look.

'I didn't know we were looking after a gerbil, Joanna,' Dad said, lying down beside her to see what he could see.

'Didn't you, darling?' Mum said. 'I thought I'd told you. It's only for a couple of days.'

11

'That's what you said about Sniff, once upon a time, I seem to remember,' he said.

Mum ignored him and twisted her head sideways a bit more to try and get a better look. She sneezed. 'Poor little soul,' she said. 'He'll get covered in dust.'

Dad lifted his head up. 'This is hopeless. I can't see a thing.' At that moment, Sal and Sniff decided to see if they could do any better, and jammed their noses under the bookcase.

'Look out!' yelled Dad. 'Don't let Sniff get to him! He'll have him for breakfast.'

'Don't be daft, Dad,' I said. 'If Sniff got a whiff of it, he'd run a mile.'

'Ben, we're talking about instinct here,' said Dad, looking dead worried. 'Once he's got his bloodlust up, he'll tear him to shreds. Not that you can blame him. It's not his fault, it's just that dogs are hunters by nature.

'Dad's right, better keep him out of it,' said Mum. 'Be quick, Ben. Grab Sniff and shut him in the kitchen.'

'And bring the flashlight,' said Dad.

'Tell you what,' said Mum, pushing herself upwards on to her knees and grabbing hold of Sniff by the scruff, '*I'll* take Sniff into the kitchen and get the flashlight; and Ben, you go into the sitting-room and just check the cage. Just in case . . .' She did the rest of the sentence slowly and silently behind her hand for me to lip-read. *'Just . . . in . . . case . . . Sal's . . . making . . . this . . . up.'* She bundled Sniff towards the kitchen.

'I think I've got gangrene,' I said.

'Very likely, dear,' said Mum. 'Hurry up, will you?'

I hobbled into the sitting-room. There under the dining table was the little wire cage from the playgroup. The door was open, the roof had been lifted off the top of the little red plastic house, so you could see that he wasn't in there and since there was no sign of him in the little bundle of hay in the corner, the gerbil had obviously hopped it.

'He's not here,' I yelled. 'The cage door's open.' I glanced round the room. Everything looked normal except that there was something a bit strange over by the music centre. There was a record on the turntable and the sleeve was lying on the floor. That wouldn't have been unusual, but this was more like half a record-sleeve. A fair bit of it had been chewed away. Someone had taken three or four records off the shelf and leaned them against the wall. In the space between the records and the wall there was a fuzzy, round thing, about the size of a grapefruit. I crawled up to them for a closer look and I could see that something had got at the sleeves of the leaning records. Thin strips of papery cardboard were hanging off them. Hey, this was brilliant! The gerbil had made a nest out of chewed record-sleeves. Dad would be dead interested in this. Last summer in Norfolk, we'd found a magpie's nest in the top branches of an elm tree that had had to be felled because of Dutch Elm disease and that had silver paper and milk bottle tops woven into it. But this was probably the first case in history of the nest being made out of cardboard and photographs of Buddy Holly and The Beach Boys.

'Dad!' I said. 'Come and have a look at this. It's made a nest.'

Dad came rushing in. 'What d'you mean, a nest?' he said.

'There in the corner,' I said, pointing. 'Well neat, eh? He's made it out of . . .'

'My God! My Sixties Collection! I don't believe it! Joanna! Joanna! I don't believe it. The destructive little rat! The rotten little vandal . . .'

'But, Dad,' I said. 'Don't you think the engineering's brilliant?'

'Wottum ickle bandle!' said Sal, arriving just before Mum who had shut Sniff and his Blood Lust in the kitchen.

'What's all the noise about?' said Mum.

'Look what your little rat has done to my Buddy Holly records! Joanna, how could you?'

'How could I what? I didn't chew them. And it's not a rat, it's a marsupial.'

14

'Rodent,' I said.

'Shut up, Ben. It's a rodent,' said Mum.

'Shuttup Ben,' said Sal.

'Rodent, marsupial, werewolf . . . whatever it is, you brought the thing home and now look what he's done. Completely ruined my Sixties records. I should have set Sniff on him. That would have fixed the little swine.'

'Only the sleeves, dear. Don't exaggerate,' said Mum, picking up one of the chewed, leaning ones. 'The records are hardly scratched. Look. And I do think you ought to calm down in front of Sal.'

'Bumbum!' said Sal who had got over-excited.

'There. Now that's enough. Let's all be calm and positive about this, shall we?' said Mum.

'You wouldn't be so calm if it had minced your Mozarts,' wailed Dad.

Mum went sort of sick-looking. 'It hasn't, has it?' She grabbed the rest of the records that had been got at and sorted through them anxiously. 'Two Buddy Hollys, a Beach Boys, a Beatles and an Elvis. *Phew!*'

'What d'you mean, *Phew*?' said Dad. 'You wouldn't be phewing if they were yours. This is infuriating.'

'I'm sorry, darling, but at least it's only been at five of them. Let's scoop him back into his cage before he does any more damage.'

'What do you mean, scoop him back?' Dad said.

'Nest and all,' said Mum.

'But he's not in the nest,' said Dad. 'He's under the bookcase tucking into two tons of Shreddies. My favourite.'

'Mini Wheats,' I said.

'Shut up, Ben. Mini Wheats. You know what I mean.'

'Shuttup Ben,' said Sal.

'Well, shouldn't you just check that he isn't in his nest?' said Mum. 'We've only got Sal's word for it that he's under the bookcase.'

'Is he in there, Ben?' Dad said to me.

'Could be, I s'pose,' I said.

'You mean you haven't checked?' said Dad, jabbing at the nest with his index finger.

'Dad, if he can shred record-sleeves,' I said, 'I wouldn't stick my finger in there to find out if he's at home.'

Dad whipped his finger away fast. Mum, Dad and I sat on the floor and looked at the nest. 'Got a pencil, Ben?' Dad said. 'Or a biro or something? Something to poke in there. . . ?' As he was speaking, Sal pushed past him, grabbed the nest in her fist and held it up in front of her nose.

'What's dat?' she said.

'Look out! Drop it, Sal! Mind your fingers!' we yelled and Dad smacked it on to the carpet.

We all stood around, waiting to see if the Thing

16

with the Razor Teeth would leap from its nest and snarl at us. But nothing happened. There wasn't a sign of movement from the nest, not a squeak.

'Back to the bookcase!' said Mum, after a pause.

Mum had found the flashlight and she shone it under the bookcase. Something had been there all right. There were little mousy droppings all over the place.

'Gone,' said Dad, gloomily, and then, 'Put that down. Ugh! Dirty!' to Sal who was concentrating on a gerbil-dropping that she was holding between her finger and thumb.

'Can't have gone far,' said Mum, brightly.

'Let's just hope he hasn't got into the desk and made a nest of those *School Friend* and *Girl* comics you've been saving,' said Dad.

'Don't be nasty,' said Mum. 'Of course he hasn't.' But she went to look, just to be on the safe side.

'OK. What exactly are we looking for?' asked Dad. 'Some vicious little hamstery, furry sort of thing, eh?'

'Don't you know what a gerbil is, Dad?' I said, shocked.

'Well . . .' said Dad. 'Not exactly. We all had normal pets when I was at school, like grass snakes and newts.'

'They're about the size of a field mouse,' I explained, 'but with much stronger back legs and a

17

longer tail. And they hop – a bit like mini kangaroos.'

'Right,' said Dad. 'Now we know what we're up against, we'd better hurry up and catch it before it does any more damage.'

'I'm going to get Sal washed and dressed,' said Mum. 'You two can search by yourselves for a bit and I'll come down and hoover up the whatnots under the bookcase.' At the mention of 'whatnots', Sal put her finger and thumb in her mouth and gave them a good suck. Mum made a face, pulled them out with a pop, grabbed hold of Sal and heaved her, squealing, upstairs towards the bathroom.

Dad and I decided that it was pretty unlikely that the gerbil had hopped up the stairs and that since the doors to the dining-room, the kitchen and the utility room were shut, it was most likely to be somewhere in the sitting-room, the hall or possibly in the downstairs loo.

Sniff started howling and scratching like crazy at the kitchen door. Maybe Dad's theory about his Killer Instinct was right.

★

The whole thing turned out to be a bit of a drag. I looked in the hall while Dad was searching the sitting-room. I shone the flashlight round the back of various bits of furniture, including the grandfather clock. I thought I was on to some evidence when I crawled under the table and found a chewed book of nursery rhymes. But there was no sign of a gerbil and when I thought about it, I realized anybody could have chewed it, so I chucked it back underneath. I had a look in the loo. Nope. Then I had the brilliant idea of looking in the cupboard under the stairs. This was really promising. If I was a gerbil, I'd have headed straight for this cupboard because there were loads of interesting things to make nests out of. I pulled out some of the stuff that was crammed in there – mops, buckets, brooms, cardboard boxes, our old hoover, some flower pots and a pile of old wellies, a couple of carrier bags full of magazines. No sign of a gerbil. Then, right at the back, there was something I recognized immediately, even though I hadn't seen it for years – a Tupperware container full of Lego. I peeled the lid off and there it was . . . all those bright, bobbly plastic bricks and wheels and windows and stuff. I put one in my mouth and lined the rough bits up with the side of my tongue, and as soon as I got the taste of it, I remembered sitting in my room listening to my tape of *The Hobbit* and making my first space-probe with docking satellite. Before I could stop myself, I was stirring among the bits, looking for a nose-cone.

'What are you up to, Ben?' Dad called, five

minutes later. He sounded a bit cheesed off. 'Any sign yet?'

'Not yet,' I shouted, quickly stuffing the half-completed model back into the container. I couldn't quite get the lid on, so I gave up and concentrated on trying to get all the junk back into the cupboard. That wasn't any easier than getting the lid on the Lego box, and in the end I found I could only shut the door by leaving the wellies, the hoover, and one of the carrier bags, a mop and a cardboard box full of cleaning stuff, outside. I dusted off my hands and went to help Dad in the sitting-room.

The sitting-room looked as if it had been hit by a hurricane. Dad had started off checking the arm-chairs and the sofa, which meant turning them over and chucking all the cushions into a heap in the middle. He'd pulled the sideboard, the corner cup-board, and the table with the computer on it, away from the wall to have a look behind them, rucking up the carpet at the same time so that it looked like a ploughed field, and now he was sitting over by the music centre surrounded by great wobbling piles of records and tapes. 'Thought I might as well get them into alphabetical order while I was at it,' he said. 'And look what I've found – my Kinks album! I thought your Uncle Peter must have pinched that. Shall we give it a whirl?' I put it on the turntable for him. Dad sat there, headbanging away to 'You Really

Come In', really enjoying himself and flicking through the pile of records beside him, when I noticed that the painted plywood board that was nailed in front of the fireplace had warped a bit so that there was a little gap at the bottom. 'Dad,' I said. 'You don't think he could have got in there, do you?'

'What?' he said. 'Oh, the gerbil. I'd forgotten about that. Well spotted, Ben,' he said. 'Pass me that screwdriver.'

'Oh, great,' I said, 'It turned up, then! That was the one we spent half of last Saturday afternoon looking for when we were trying to fix the radio-alarm! Where'd you find it?'

'Down the back of the settee,' Dad said, gritting his teeth and digging the end of it between the plywood and the chimney breast. I got my fingers under an edge he'd got loose and we both wiggled and tugged and heaved at the board. There was a shrieking of nails and suddenly, without warning, the plywood fell away and as it did so, there was a flump, and a massive wodge of soot hit the grate and splashed up into our faces. A choking black cloud sent us running out into the hall.

'That does it!' said Dad, as we dodged out into the hall and he slammed the sitting-room door shut behind us. 'No good fiddling about any more. This demands firm and decisive action . . .' He suddenly focused on me and nearly jumped out of his skin.

'Good grief, Ben! You look as if you've been down a coal mine!'

'You should see *your* face,' I said. His eyes and teeth looked amazingly white against the black. 'And your pyjamas.'

Dad wiped his hand across his forehead, leaving smeary grey smudges like worry-lines in the soot. 'Your mother's going to go bananas when she sees this lot,' he whispered, waving his thumb at the sitting-room door. 'Right. Only one thing for it. We'll have to find that pest in a hurry. We'll just have to get Sniff after him before he does any more damage.'

'OK, but what happens if he . . . you know . . . gets his Blood Lust up and goes for him?' I whispered back.

'Well, what we'll have to do is . . . we'll keep a really close eye on him in case he gets savage. OK? We won't let him attack him or anything. We'll just let him sniff him out and then we'll grab the little blighter and bung him back in the cage. Right? Quick as we can now. And give me your pyjama top,' he added, wrestling his own off. 'We'll bung them in the washing machine. Come to think of it, you'd better give me the trousers as well.'

We crunched naked along the hall, through the Mini Wheats, made a quick detour to the utility room to dump our sooty jimjams, and headed for the kitchen. When he heard us coming, Sniff banged his front paws on the kitchen door just to remind us that he was there and ready to mangle any pesky gerbil that got in his way, and then he jumped back out of the way to let Dad open it. Dad turned the handle and gave the door a shove. Sniff came pounding into the doorway, took one look at Dad and me, let out a horrible 'Yike' and dived under the table with his tail between his legs. We peered underneath and there he was, curled up in his box with his paw over his head. You could just make out the white of his eye where he was trying to peek.

When Dad clapped his hands, one ear came up, but otherwise he didn't move. 'Come on, Sniff, let's go. Seek him. Find the gerbil. Where is he?'

Nothing, not a twitch. Sniff stayed put, growling quietly to himself. 'Come on, Sniff,' I said. 'Stop mucking about. Find the mousy. Fetch.'

'I think he thinks it's a trap,' said Dad. 'It's only us,' he said to Sniff, 'Dad and Ben. Look.' He smeared a bit more of the muck off round his mouth and nose with his fingers, but Sniff still looked *well* nervous. 'Blast,' said Dad. 'It must be the soot that's got him scared and we haven't got time to wash.'

'Try this,' I said. I grabbed a paper bag out of the kitchen drawer, poked a couple of eyeholes in it with my finger and plonked it on over my head and face.

23

Sniff took his paw off his head and rolled his eyes at me.

'I s'pose he does look a bit more relaxed about that,' Dad agreed, and in a couple of secs he'd sorted out a paper bag for himself, poked in the eyeholes and pulled it on. Sniff started to pant and shiver. 'Yes, he's definitely loosening up a bit. Get him a few Doggie Chocs, that should clinch it.'

I laid a trail of Doggie Chocs from Sniff's box right round the kitchen and out through the door. Normally he would have been hoovering them up, but all he did now was to shiver and whine.

'Oh, this is ridiculous,' said Dad. 'He's gone all neurotic. We'll just have to grab him and get him on his feet. You grab that end.'

It was a heck of a job lifting him out of his box, because he'd decided to go limp. Finally, with a lot of huffing and puffing, that sounded even worse with a paper bag over your head, we got him out and on to the tiles. In spite of the fact that he was lying with his nose against a Doggie Choc, he made no attempt even to give it a lick.

'Only one thing for it, in that case. A tug of war with the blanket. Pass it over, Ben.'

I pulled his smelly old blanket out of the box. That did the trick all right. He couldn't resist a tug of war. He jumped up straight away with a woof and a shake, wagging his tail and barging the kitchen chairs

about. He got his teeth into the corner of his blanket, braced his back legs, hunched up his shoulders and heaved, backing off, shaking his head wildly and growling like a tiger. I tried to get a firm grip on the tiles with my bare feet, but slipped on a Doggie Choc and went down on my bare backside with a *well* nasty whack. 'YOW!'

'Right, that's more like it! Let's go. Let's go seek!' Dad said, ignoring my agony and trying to take advantage of Sniff's new-found energy.

Something caught my attention among the cut-up sweaters and scarves and squeaky toys that lined Sniff's box. I stopped rubbing my rear end and looked closer. Something small with reddish-brown fur and a pointy face was stirring slowly and eye-balling me. 'Get the cage, Dad,' I said. 'I've found the gerbil. Sniff's been lying on it.'

'WHAAATT!!??'

'He must have been lying on it all the time we were turning everything out.'

By now, Sniff had recovered enough from his fright to become aware of the trail of Doggie Chocs, and he was slurping away with his long rubbery tongue. Once he'd got the taste, the only thing in the world that mattered to him was the next Doggie Choc. When Dad nipped along to the sitting-room to fetch the cage, he didn't even bother to look up. 'So much for our worries about Sniff going mad with bloodlust and tearing the poor little thing to pieces,' he said. 'He didn't even notice it when he was tucked up in bed with it!'

'Too blinking dozy,' I said, holding the gerbil up by its tail to examine it before lowering it gently on to the sawdust and sunflower seeds at the bottom of its cage. 'He must have been lying on it all night. But it looks OK now. I think it was just dazed.'

'Half-suffocated I should imagine, with about half a ton of dog lying on it,' said Dad. He turned and gave Sniff a good scratch and a pat. 'Well done, boy,' he said. 'Practically demolished my Beach Boys, that little pest.'

'How are you guys doing down there?' We froze as Mum's voice echoed down the stairwell. Instinctively, I reached up to take the paper bag off and then down again to cover my embarrassment, but Dad flapped wildly at me to warn me about giving away how sooty we were before we'd had chance to clear up a bit. We heard the familiar bump-bump-bump of Sal's bottom as she came down in front of Mum. We heard her rootling among the stuff I'd left outside the hall cupboard and Mum's voice going into banana-mode. 'And what the heck is all this . . . and these black footprints and. . . ?'

'Hey, guess what! We found the gerbil!' said Dad, stepping out with the cage held in front of him like a shield. I imagined the smile like a day-glo corn on the cob that was hidden behind the paper bag. He was desperately trying to distract her before she stepped into the sitting-room.

'Sniff found him, actually,' I chipped in.

Mum looked at us as though we'd both just crawled out of a flying saucer. 'What *are* you guys up to?'

'Hygiene,' I said. It was the first thing that came into my head. 'You have to be careful about breathing germs on gerbils.'

Mum shook her head. 'I can believe this of *you*, Ben, but why a grown man should take all his clothes off and stick a paper bag over his head beats me. You'd better put something on and get those bags off

27

before Sal sees you. I don't want you giving her ideas like that – pulling things over her face. It's dangerous,' She grabbed a dustpan and brush, pulled the door closed as she stepped out into the hall among the Mini Wheats.

'Why don't we all have some meckmus?' called Dad through the door, desperately trying to save the situation.

'Fine,' said Mum sharply. 'I'll sweep some up for you, shall I?'

'Good idea,' called Dad, whipping off his paper bag, rushing over to the sink and sticking his head under the tap. He signalled frantically at me to do the same.

'Where was he, the gerbil, by the way?' Mum wanted to know as she swept.

'In the kitchen, actually,' Dad replied – in a muffled, under water sort of way.

'Really?' said Mum. 'Thank the Lord for that. I had this horrible thought that he might have got stuck up the chimney or something. No Sal, leave those things alone. I've got to get them all back in the cupboard somehow. We'll just set you up something to do in the sitting-room for a minute while I sort things out in the hall, shall we?'

When we heard that, we knew we'd had it, and Dad and I stood frozen, with cold water running down the back of our necks and Fairy Liquid stinging our eyes. It was still only just gone seven o'clock in the morning, and I had already stubbed my toe, been choked by soot, bruised my bum and been half-drowned. Half an hour before, I had got up in the hope of finding a bit of peace. Now, here I was, standing dripping on to the kitchen tiles with Dad, both of us with our fingers in our ears, waiting for an explosion.

'RRRALPH!' said Sniff. He meant that he'd come to the end of the trail of Doggie Chocs. I knew exactly how he felt.

Sniff Comes Scrumping

It was a fair cop really, though I didn't think so at the time – hanging by the seat of my track suit pants from a barbed wire fence.

Munford had started it when we were running round the cross country circuit. He's only a skinny little kid but he had more breath than me as we jogged along the rough track that led past the orchard.

'Great cherries,' he panted, jerking his head towards the trees on our left to show me where he got them from.

I was dodging about, trying not to twist my ankle in the deep ruts made by tractor wheels, and too knackered to answer.

'Had a load of 'em last night, me and Bowra.'

'Get out,' I gasped. I didn't believe him. Everyone knew about Bullock, the big bloke with a droopy moustache and cropped hair, who lived in the cottage we'd passed a bit further back up the track. He was always hanging about, in his garden or in the greenhouses in the nursery opposite the orchard, glaring at kids or shouting at them to keep to the track and off the edge of his field. He'd have your guts for garters if he caught you trying to scrump his cherries.

The week before, Year One had been sent on a training run and Bullock had had a go at Beggs for stopping by his fence just along from the greenhouses. Beggs had got a stitch and he'd just happened to stop by the fence for a bit of a rest. He bent over – like you do when you get a stitch – and he saw these two cherries just lying there in the grass. He picked them up and old Bullock came out of one of the greenhouses and went mad at him. Beggs was still shaking when he told us about it in the changing room.

'He's been in the army and all, Bullock,' said Beggs, rubbing his trembling knees with a towel.

'He has,' said Wallace, in case we didn't believe him. He's Beggs's mate so he was sticking up for him.

'He told me he's learnt all different ways of killing people with his bare hands . . .'

'Like pressing on your nerves and that, and giving you karate chops,' added Wallace.

'And he said to pass it on to anyone else who tried scrumping cherries.'

'But he wasn't,' said Wallace, 'were you, Beggsie? He just *found* two, lying on the ground.'

I looked at Munford's skinny legs now as he cut in front of me to avoid a particularly deep tractor rut. I couldn't believe a couple of stick insects like him and Bowra would have the bottle to touch *one* of those cherries – let alone a whole load. Anyway, the thought of Bullock's strong fingers pressing on one of my nerves, maybe right in the salt-cellar, made me put on a bit of a spurt and overtake Munford, even though I was knackered, so I didn't say anything else about it to him till dinner time back at school.

*

'You and *Bowra*? You must be joking!' I shouted above the noise in the canteen.

Munford was pushing a forkful of mashed potatoes into his mouth and reaching for his plums and custard. His hair was still wet from the shower.

'About two pounds each, I reckon,' he said, not waiting for the potatoes to go down before he started on his pud. 'Big 'uns and all.'

'Pull the other one,' I said.

'Ask Bowra,' said Munford. 'Here he comes.' Bowra had worked his way past the prefect on duty and up to the front of the dinner queue by pretending he was on choir practice. He was nearly as skinny as Munford and a bit taller. He had neat wavy hair and wore proper school uniform, even the shoes. He was always getting away with things because he looked such a square. But scrumping off Bullock? *Bowra?*

'Hear you've been scrumping,' I said as he squeezed on to the bench in between Munford and a spotty kid.

Bowra looked at Munford. 'I told him about last night,' said Munford, and Bowra grinned. 'How many pounds of cherries you reckon we got off old Bullock? Couple?'

'At least,' gloated Bowra, taking the top off his meat pie and scooping some of the brown stuff into his mouth. 'Why? Doesn't Moore believe you?'

'Doesn't reckon we've got the bottle,' said Munford.

'Jealous, that's all,' said Bowra, showing his little teeth. ''Cause we've got more guts than him.'

'I don't go round stealing,' I said.

'Scrumping's not stealing,' said Munford. 'Specially not from a big misery like Bullock.'

'Anyway,' said Bowra, 'you don't have to keep the cherries if you don't want to. All you've got to do to prove you've got some bottle is – get into the orchard, fill your pockets, bring 'em in to school to show me and Munford. After that you can . . .'

'. . . leave 'em outside Bullock's back door,' chipped in Munford. 'That way everybody's happy.'

'How come I have to prove anything? Where's *your* evidence?' I said.

'In here,' said Munford, pushing back from the table so he could pat his stomach.

'Just forget it if you don't believe us,' grinned Bowra.

'So where did you get in the orchard?' I said.

'That's for us to know and you to find out,' they said together as if they'd been practising. They thought they were *so* cool.

*

I asked Max if he wanted to come with me – just to show Munford and Bowra. He said he didn't fancy it and I didn't push him, but I was dead annoyed because – well mainly because Max is meant to be my mate and, well, I couldn't stop thinking about their stupid grinning faces.

Thurston told me it was just a wind-up and the whole thing was puerile. That was bad enough, but what really got me was that having said *he* wouldn't sink to the level of Munford and Bowra, he told me I'd be an idiot to try it on my own. 'And as Munford and Bowra have demonstrated,' he smirked, 'it is clearly a job for *two* idiots.'

'Right, you lot,' I thought. 'Right.'

*

'Just off doing a bit of training for the three million metres,' I called from the hall. It was about six o'clock and we weren't having supper till late because Mum was finishing an essay for her Open University course and it was Dad's turn to cook.

'Well take Sniff with you,' called Dad. 'He could do with a good r . . .'

I slammed the front door and legged it. Didn't want Sniff charging about, giving the game away. If I was going to sneak past old Bullock and into his orchard, it was going to take some quiet and crafty work. Sniff is dead crafty sometimes, but quiet – never!

I could have gone by bike, but the whole point of jogging was to give me a proper excuse for being seen near the orchard. Trouble was, it was even further from our house than it was if you set off from school, so I was well knackered by the time I reached Bullock's cottage. I stuck my chest out as I went by the garden gate, trying to look dead athletic. No sign of him in the garden. I relaxed a bit and trotted on towards the greenhouses, getting up on my tiptoes as I got nearer the orchard, in case he was about somewhere. Then I slowed to a stop and tried to control my panting and the thumping of my heart. Still no sign or sound of anybody.

I risked a quick look to my left, hoping to see a gap in the barbed wire fence, but there was no way I could see myself wiggling through it or under it. The only gate into it was right back close to the cottage where anybody could see you going through, and there wasn't any other gap . . . unless . . .

Right up against the fence, about twenty metres along from where I was standing, there was this big old oak tree, with a thick, twisty sort of trunk. If I could somehow climb it – I took a closer look to check – I might be able to work my way across a branch that hung right over one of the biggest cherry trees. With my weight bending it, it would come down like a drawbridge. That way I'd be able to get a couple of pocketfuls of cherries without having to set foot in the orchard. That would show all the cocky so-and-sos who reckoned I'd never make it. Ace!

The trouble was, the lowest branch on the track side was miles out of reach. Still, round the other side of the tree, close to the fence, there was loads of ivy tangled round the trunk. By walking up the barbed wire with my feet and heaving up on the ivy with my hands, I was soon up on the top strand of the fence. From there I got both hands and one foot hooked round a good strong branch. I struggled up and over and rolled till I got one leg on each side of it. I managed to stand up, and worked my way round the trunk to the drawbridge-branch. I straddled it with my back to the trunk, and by pushing down with my hands and shuffling my bum at the same time, hopped towards the end of the branch and towards the centre of the big cherry tree. As I got nearer – just as I'd planned – I felt myself being lowered gently within reach of some of the darkest, shiniest, juiciest looking cherries I've ever seen – bunches and bunches of them.

I stretched down, feeling the branch move a bit like a boat on the water, and just managed to touch a couple with the tips of my fingers. I held my breath and stretched harder, shaking with the strain. Just-a-cent-i-met-re-fur-ther . . .

RRRAALLPH!!

I snapped up like an elastic band. The branch swayed and bucked and tipped me off sideways. I scissored my legs, grabbed at bunches of leaves with my hands, and hung on like mad.

RRRAALPH!' I heard, 'RRRAALPH! RRRA-ALPH! RRRAALPH!'

I concentrated on staying alive and somehow managed not to fall. Then there was a lot of scratching at the trunk of the oak tree, and growling and whining so loud that old Bullock *had* to have heard it!

'Sniff! What the heck are you doing here!' I hissed through my gritted teeth. He must have got through the back fence and picked up my scent across the Rec.

So that was it. I was dead. Bullock was probably on his way, working out which nerve he was going to press right now. My only hope was to get Sniff away before Bullock worked out exactly where all the racket was coming from. Somehow I wriggled myself round and up on my branch again till I was facing the trunk and fence. It was dead slow going at first, because the branch kept dipping and rocking. Then I hitched my way along it as quickly as I could until I had hold of the trunk of the oak, and straight away I started feeling with my feet for the lower branches. 'Buzz off, Sniff!' I hissed. 'Go home! Go find Sal! Leave me alone!'

As soon as he heard my voice, he started barking and scraping and whining even louder. I broke off a twig and chucked it at him. It missed, but he grabbed it, shook it about, tossed it aside and started barking for more. In the few seconds it took him to fetch the twig, it was quiet enough to hear the sound of voices – one a woman's and the other so deep and rumbly that it had to be the voice of a trained killer.

They must have been working right at the back of the greenhouse that was farthest from the track, when the barking started. By the time they finally realized that something was going on at the far end of the orchard and started running in that direction disaster number two had struck. I'd busted off a long stick and tried to reach down so that I could poke Sniff with it – to show him I meant business about him shutting up and buzzing off home. It had almost worked. He was looking dead thoughtful about all the hissing and waving going on over his head, and he might have taken the hint – except I suddenly lost my balance and fell backwards out of the tree.

I let out a heck of a shriek, certain I was about to bust my neck, when all of a sudden the ground stopped rushing towards me. There was this ripping,

cranging sound, and with a jerk that nearly snapped my head off, something grabbed the seat of my pants. I'd got snagged by the top strand of the barbed wire fence. I came diving down head first before being hoisted up again by the wire. I can faintly remember Sniff going 'Yike' and belting off down the track like a greyhound while I bobbed up and down like a yoyo for a bit.

Seconds later, two meaty hands reached up and got a grip on my arms and shoulders. I struggled and shouted as much as I could to stop Bullock getting a death-grip on me, but it was no good; those hands were like vices. The big red upside-down face below me went all creased with the strain. It reminded me of the picture of the Minotaur hanging in the Junior Library.

'Keep still!' boomed the deep voice.

'Get him to straighten his legs,' came the other voice, the woman's.

'Straighten your legs, boy,' ordered the deep voice. I didn't need telling again and did as I was told. In a couple of shakes, I'd been dragged out of my track suit pants and was sitting in my running shorts on the grass by the fence. I started to shake worse than Beggs.

'Right, we'd better sort you out,' said Bullock. The dagger tattooed on his forearm had a snake winding up it and a banner underneath that said 'Death or

Glory'. He stepped back. Whatever he was going to do to me, he needed a run up. I put my arms over my head, knowing they wouldn't be much protection.

'You're all right now, lad,' said the woman, not unkindly. 'He's gone.'

No he blinking hasn't, I thought. *He's still there. I can hear him panting.*

'Nasty sneaky things! They want chainin' up!' roared Bullock.

'Well he's long gone now, you're all right, don't you fret,' said the woman.

Long gone? What was she on about - *gone?* He was right beside her, stretching up with his huge arms. What was he after? Was he going to break off a branch to whop me with? No he was . . . getting my track suit trousers untangled from the barbed wire!

'That was smart thinking, boy, nipping up that tree,' rumbled Bullock, squatting in front of me and holding out the trousers. His droopy moustache was twitching with emotion. 'They train you to do that in the army if you're out in the open, like, if you're threatened by a predator. You done well getting up there.'

'He'd done *very* well, ditten he?' said the woman, kneeling on the grass beside me and pushing the hair out of my eyes. 'He'd have had you, that dog. Nasty, big hairy brute by the look of it. Did he bite you at all?'

41

I shook my head.

'Oh, just look at your track suit! Great big holes in the seat! Ruined that is! What a shame. Training for something are you?' asked the woman.

'Tell you what, Mum,' said Bullock. 'What about a couple of pound of cherries to take home, like. That'll cheer him up a bit, wunnit?'

'Would you like that? For being such a brave lad? And then Mr Bullock'll drop you off home in the car. All right?'

I said that would be very nice but not to bother about the car. I'd rather finish my training run. And when they asked if I wasn't worried about the nasty dog, I said no, I'd risk it. So they looked at each other and shook their heads, meaning: *What a wonderful, brave young man. Pity you don't get more of his type around these days!*

★

'And then they said to drop in any time I was passing,' I said. This was before registration, by the lockers, the following day. 'They said for me to just – you know – pop into the orchard any time I was passing and help myself to cherries. Wicked, eh? That's only till the end of the week, mind you – they're picking them for the market at the weekend. Oh yes, they're really nice, Mr Bullock and his mum, once you get to know them.'

Munford looked at Bowra and Bowra looked at Munford and then they both looked at me . . . and at the cherries in the *Bullock's Commercial Growers* bag in my locker.

'And you were just – like – *running* past?' Bowra asked.

'That's it,' I said. 'It all happened in a matter of seconds. Anyway, Mr Bullock was dead impressed.'

So were Bowra and Munford, by the look of them. It must be the way I tell 'em – but they weren't laughing, that's for sure.

Course, they would have been if they'd heard the whole story, but I'd changed it a bit. In the new version, I'd saved Mr Bullock's mum from this vicious dog and been treated as a real hero. Well, it wasn't any fancier than Munford and Bowra's load of nonsense. Neither of them would have dreamt of going anywhere *near* the orchard, not after what happened to Beggs. I s'pose I knew that all along really.

The important thing was not to let Max and Thurston in on the actual facts. Or the actual cherries, come to think of it. If Thurston knew about Sniff being there, my nose would have got *well* rubbed in it, especially after what he'd said about it being a job for two idiots.

He can be dead cutting like that, Thurston.

Sniff and the Sensitive Cousin

I didn't say anything when my cousin Jason tripped me up outside the lounge just after we arrived at Aunty Pat's. I kept quiet about his gross T-shirt. I understood about him eating the only three Jaffa Cakes on the plate. I tried to keep my mind on having a good time on the beach later.

Mum had given me this lecture about Jason having growth-hormone injections for about fifteen hours on the way down to Aunty Pat's in the car. I had to be really understanding about how short he was and everything, because he was the sensitive type.

Sensitive! Ha ha.

I *did* say one thing when we went up to his room, when the first thing he did was drop his jeans and show me his bum. It looked just an ordinary bum but he told me his dad had to put the needle in there twice a week, once in each cheek. I said 'Wow', which I thought was just about enough without making a big thing out of it, because Mum had said not to draw attention to his problem and all that. So then he pushed up his bedroom window, climbed on to the window-sill with his feet dangling down, and peed right across the gap between his house and the one next door – right on to the roof! That was something else I kept quiet about.

'Try it,' he said to me, climbing back in. I said no thanks. I told him I'd only just been, which was true, but the fact was I thought it was bit weird doing it out of the window. Besides, I'd never have got it across that gap. That roof was miles away.

Jason was obviously well chuffed to have found something he could do that I couldn't, so soon after I'd arrived, and he kept looking for other ways of making himself look big in front of me.

'Ever been to an arcade?' he asked, starting to bounce in the middle of his bed like a trampoline. 'Good bed, eh?' he added. 'Try it.' He stuck out his bottom lip and blew so that he parted the hair in his fringe. It was a habit he had.

'What sort of arcade?' I said, getting into a rhythm with him. The bed creaked and clanged.

'Amusement. Loads of electronic games, slot machines, all that.'

There was a double yell from downstairs, so we had two more bounces and stopped.

'I've been loads of times. They're fantastic. I'll take you if you like. Got any money?'

'Not much,' I said.

'We're gonna need loads,' he said.

'I heard you're not allowed into amusement arcades on your own until you're sixteen,' I said. 'So how come they let you in?'

He tucked in his chin and took a big gulp of air. Then he let out the loudest, rippingest burp. GEEERRRRRFF. 'Charm,' he said. He wouldn't go into details.

★

The morning after we arrived it was bit chilly. I told Jason I quite fancied going down the beach, to have a look round, but I didn't feel like swimming.

'What's up with you?' he said.

'It's freezing,' I said.

'Get out!' he said. 'I go in colder than this, don't I Dad?'

Uncle Dave gave a little nod and a wink, to show he agreed that Jason was dead hard. 'Don't let him wear you out, Ben,' he said. 'He's on the go all the time, that boy of ours.'

'All the time,' said Aunty Pat, in case I didn't believe him.

We managed to get out without Sniff or Sal realizing we'd gone. Jason made it clear he didn't think much of Sniff and didn't want him around. He said he was stupid, which is true in a way, but I don't think you should go around saying things like that to people's faces. Anyway, I'd seen Sniff with Sal from an upstairs window, going into Uncle Dave's greenhouse. Sal had her bucket and spade with her, so I guessed they'd be busy for a while.

I put on my swimming trunks, T-shirt and trainers, and rolled up a towel. When we got outside, Jason, who was only wearing trunks, said, 'Leave your shoes on the porch. Only trippers wear shoes.'

I didn't want to look like a tripper, but when we got to the bottom of Cliffe Avenue, we had to cross this wide road called The Royal Esplanade that was covered in sharp loose chippings. 'Doesn't hurt!' Jason said, and charged across the road. I set off, hobbling and tiptoeing and trying to look casual but it was well painful. Jason stood on the pavement at the other side laughing his head off. 'Tripper!'

When I finally got to the pavement, he said, 'That's the steps down to the beach along there. You can walk down that way if you haven't got the bottle to come down the cliff with me.' He unrolled his towel, threw it round his shoulders like a cape, and tied two corners under his chin. '*Duh-daaah* – Superman! See. Do your towel like that.' Anybody would have thought he'd invented the idea.

There was drop of about fifteen or twenty metres down to the promenade. At the top of the cliff there was a bit of fenced-off lawn and rock-garden. Jason obviously had plans to go over the fence, across the lawn and straight down. 'Watch your feet on these railings,' he said. 'I knew a kid once got his feet stuck in them. Fell forward and broke both legs. Snapped one of his feet off.'

'What do you mean, 'off'?' I said, secretly wondering how far it was to the steps. 'You mean *right* off?'

'Well . . . dangling,' Jason said, heaving himself up and over. The fence wasn't all that high.

'Yeah, same sort of thing happened to my friend Max,' I said. (I just had to hope Jason never got the chance to check this out.)

'What?'

'Lost one of his feet in an accident. He got gangrene.'

'Oh, right,' said Jason, peeved. He also looked a bit narked that I got over the fence without any trouble. 'Over this way.'

Once you crossed the lawn and the rock-garden at the top of the cliff, you could see that it was no big deal to get down.

It wasn't really like a cliff at all. It was more like a steep bank, most of it grassed over, but with a pathway down to the promenade that had obviously been made by millions of people using that way down as a short cut. It was bit skiddy but no real hassle.

It was before nine o'clock, so there was hardly anyone about except an old couple sitting in their coats and hats on the long seat that went right the way along the promenade at the bottom of the 'cliff'. They were busy pouring tea out of a thermos flask, so they didn't notice us until we thumped down on to the seat next to them and bounced from there on to the promenade. They jumped up and the old lady put her hand on her chest and said 'Oo, mah good Gawd!'

'Where did you spring from?' said the old man.

'Down the cliff. Don't worry, we're locals, we always come down the hard way,' Jason said.

'Oo-er,' said the old lady. 'You want to mind yer don't break yer necks.'

'It's all right if you know what you're doing,' said Jason.

'Ain't you chilly, son?' said the old man. Jason was a bit blue round the lips. I was chilly too, but they obviously thought he was cute, being such a short kid.

'Used to it,' said Jason. 'Aren't we, Lennie?'

I looked round for a second. Then I realized he was talking to me. I don't know why he changed my name. Maybe he wanted to pretend I belonged to him, like a dog or something, I don't know. 'Me and Lennie are going for a swim. You can watch if you like.'

'Oo-er,' said the old lady, impressed and pulling her warm coat tighter round her. I looked across the sand at the sea. It was grey and choppy. Not surprising there was no one else on the beach.

Jason stretched out his arms and started running towards the edge of the prom. He banked to the left (*'Eeee-oww!'*), banked to the right (*'Eeee-oww!'*) so that his towel flew up behind him and then launched himself off the edge down on to the beach. It was quite a jump for a titchy kid. Even I nearly winded myself as I hit the cold sand beside him but he was up and running towards the breakwater that stretched about a hundred metres out into the sea. At first the sand was soft but suddenly it was almost as bad as crossing the road had been, because at the high tide line there was a mound of dried seaweed, broken shells and pebbles. Still, the old couple were watching and I didn't want to be a tripper so I tried to stay cool and keep going as if my feet weren't killing me. It helped a bit going *'Eee-oww'*.

Jason dumped his towel on the sand and then

scrambled on to the breakwater. When I took off my T-shirt, it was so freezing cold, my chest went all bumpy like a fresh-chilled chicken. Still, I nipped after Jason and jumped up after him on to the breakwater. I wasn't ready for how slippery it was, and I'd only taken one step forward when I crashed down on my knees and from there on to my chest. When I got up, Jason was laughing his head off. I was covered in green slime, right down my body. The stiff breeze made me break out all over in goose pimples and I started to shudder.

'Have a nice trip, tripper? Let's go!' said Jason. He turned and he was off again, moving like a fast tightrope walker. He was obviously used to it. There was nothing for it but to follow and I staggered after him, feet and arms shooting everywhere.

When I finally caught up with him, we were only about thirty metres from this thing like a lamppost, with a rusty iron shade on, that marked the end of the breakwater, and our feet were actually in the sea. It was freezing. Suddenly, Jason took a deep breath, squatted right down till his knees were in his chest, and pushed himself off. He kicked like mad for about ten seconds and then he was jumping up and down about four or five metres from the breakwater, gasping and shouting. 'I had my eyes open all the time!' he yelled. He wiped them with the palms of his hands to demonstrate. The water wasn't deep at all, because it only came up to his chin and he started bouncing off the bottom towards me again, splashing and making a lot of noise. He was making all the noise partly because it was so cold and partly to cover up the fact that *he couldn't swim a stroke!* It was all flash!

I was getting a bit fed up with Jason trying to impress me all the time, so I thought I'd show him something worth watching. 'Er, Jason, Jason,' I called, trying to time it between splashes. He stopped and looked up. 'Hang on a sec,' I said, and flexed my knees. I got the best grip with my toes that I could on the edge of the breakwater, leaned forward and stretched my arms as I cut the surface of the water in a pretty smart racing dive. The cold smacked the breath out of me, but I managed twenty of the fastest, foamingest butterfly strokes I could muster, hardly rising for air, somersault-turned into a crawl and churned back towards where Jason was standing. As soon as I touched the breakwater, I pushed off it again with my feet barely feeling the prickly barnacles that dug into my skin – and backstroked twenty or thirty metres in a blinding storm of white water. I made the run back towards Jason with a nice snorting breaststroke, finally leaping up, slapping the top of the wall under the surface of the water and twisting right round so that I finished up sitting next to where Jason was shivering and dripping. Only he wasn't looking. He was facing the other way, pretending to be dead interested in something on the other side of the breakwater.

He stepped over me, pushing my head forward and almost shoving me back into the sea, and set off back towards the beach. I caught up with him as he was drying himself with his towel, standing on my T-shirt. I pulled it out from under him and said 'Oy!' but all he said was, 'You were dead lucky there, you know.'

'What are you talking about?' I said through my rattling teeth.

'Jellyfish,' he said, knotting his towel under his chin Superman-style again, before trotting off and *ee-owing* his way back to where the old couple were sitting. I heard him explaining to them about Portuguese Men o' War and how they're the deadliest kind of jellyfish and how they have long sort of testacles that wave about and sting you and how if you get them wrapped round your head you'll die.

'Oo-er! said the old lady.

'You're talkin' about tentacles, you are,' said the old man.

'That's what I said,' said Jason. 'Long stringly stingy things. I saw them when I was swimming with my eyes open. That's why I got out. I told Lennie, but he never heard me. Otherwise I would prob'ly have swum for about half an hour or something.'

'You look ever so cold,' the old lady said. 'You wanna git sumfin' warm on.'

'It's OK, we're locals,' said Jason. 'Let's go, Lennie.' And he scrambled up on to the seat, got a grip on a tuft of grass and hauled himself up on the chalk cliff-track. I followed, and as we reached the rock-garden at the top, I heard the old man say, 'Plucky little chap, en he?' and I knew he wasn't talking about me.

*

I don't know what it was about Jason but he had a way of getting you following him about. He was kind of weird but interesting, if you know what I mean. For example, he nicked fifty pence out of Aunty Pat's purse when we went back to the house and got changed. Then he took me to this sweetshop and bought a load of sherbet lemons which he said were his favourite. When we came out of the shop, he wouldn't eat any. He waited till we'd got round the corner from the shop and there was no one about, and he laid three sherbet lemons in the gutter in a row and stamped on them.

'What did you do that for?' I asked.

'For luck,' he explained. 'Otherwise there'd be a

curse on them, and besides, we need some more money for the arcades.'

The way he talked about the slot machines and the Space Invader-type games and the racing machines and everything made it sound great. So when he came up with this plan for getting money to spend in the arcades, I said I'd give it a go.

★

We'd nearly finished lunch and I was trying to dig the last bits of chocolate pud out of the dents in the bottom of the carton when Jason elbowed me in the ribs.

'All *right*,' I said out of the side of my mouth. Dad was looking at the What's On section of *The Isle of Thanet Gazette* with Uncle Dave, trying to pick somewhere to go in the evening. Jason had dug me in the ribs because he reckoned Dad had gone into Uh-huh mode.

I thought it might be worth a try. 'Dad . . . '

'Uh-huh.'

'Me and Jace have been thinking.'

'Uh-huh.' Rustle rustle.

'You know what you were saying in the car about historical remains round the coast here . . . ?'

'Uh-huh.' Dad's hand started groping around for his cup. I pushed it into his grip and he hung on to it for a bit while he peered at the page in front of him.

'Concert at the Winter Gardens tonight Joanna,' he said thoughtfully.

I said, dead casually, 'So we thought we'd hire a metal detector and go down the beach and have a look for some . . . like coins and Roman helmets and stuff.'

'Uh-huh.'

'And they're only £7.50 a day plus deposit. Well cheap, eh?'

'Uh-uh,' said Dad. Same tone of voice but was that 'Uh-*huh*' or 'Uh-*uh*'? Keep going, keep going.

'So it's only £17.50 altogether and you get a tenner back when you take the thing back to the shop.'

'No chance,' said Dad. He rolled up the paper and thwacked me on the head with it. What a bummer. Aunty Pat must have lifted Sal down from her chair because as I ducked out of the way of a second thwack, Sal banged me on the eyebrow with her spoon.

'Pam!' she yelled.

'Ow! Watch it!' I yelled back. 'That hurt!'

'That's not a spam,' Jason said. 'This is a spam. See?' And he spammed me right in the middle of the forehead with the flat of his hand.

Suddenly I got another ding with the spoon, bang on the knuckle of the hand I was holding against my eye. 'Pam!' Sal yelled.

56

'Sal! Pack it in!' I said.

Dad picked her up, but she managed to kick me in the ear on the way. As soon as Dad got into the action, Sniff burrowed under the table, got a claw caught up in the fringe of the tablecloth, dragging loads of knives and forks and plates on top of himself before he got his teeth into Dad's cardigan. It always gets him going if he thinks people are fighting.

I just might have got something out of Dad for that kick in the ear, but now that Sniff had done a loopy, Mum had a go at Dad for setting a bad example, and there was obviously no way he was going to listen to me now. I had one more try anyway, just in case.

'£7.50's not much for something really educational, is it?'

'Do shut up, Ben,' said Mum, kneeling to pick up the things off the floor. 'And buzz off. You had all that money that Grandad gave you, plus extra pocket money, and if you've squandered it in two days — tough.'

Jason looked at me with a 'What money?' look on his face, so I said 'Oh, *Mum*. You know I'm saving that up for a mountain bike.'

'Tough,' she said again. 'You'll have to go down to the beach and dig with your buckets and spades like everybody else, won't you?' Some holiday this was turning out to be. No point in going down the arcades with no dosh.

'And take Sniff with you. See if you can wear him out,' Dad said. That was it. Straight away, Sniff started to whine and yelp and then he ran and chucked himself at the front door.

Lumbered.

*

'At least we didn't get stuck with Sal as well,' I said to Jason who was standing with his legs apart on the beach, bucketing sand between them on to a pile behind him. 'After that mess she made in your dad's greenhouse this morning they could easily have sent her out with us.'

Jason carried on bucketing. He wasn't making anything, just showing some little kids nearby, who were quietly building a sandcastle, how an expert goes to work. They just carried on with their own thing, filling their buckets, patting the sand flat with their spades and tipping the contents up into neat little mounds. The tide was out and there was a game of cricket going on down on the hard sand, below the high water line. Sniff was hanging about over there, running off with the ball whenever he could get hold of it. Any minute, the players were going to get fed up and start looking for his owner to take him away.

'You didn't even see the point, did you, Dumbo?' said Jason.

'Of what?'

'We weren't actually going to *hire* the metal detector, we were just gonna spend the £7.50, and then we'd have just gathered up a few bits of old junk, like cans and stuff, and said that's all we could find but thanks very much for the very rewarding experience. Get it? You didn't even have to mention the deposit money! That was what put him off.'

'I thought the idea was to *find* some money,' I said.

'Oh yeah, very likely. We were gonna find over £7.50 in one afternoon and still have time to take the metal detector back to the shop *and* have a go in the arcades? Do us a favour. And what with you being too tight to spend your money, we're stuck down here mucking about in the sand like a couple of trippers.'

'Well, I quite fancy taking a look in those rock-pools right over there,' I said. 'We might find some shrimps or a hermit crab or something. I've never actually seen a hermit crab.'

'Waste of time,' said Jason.

'Well what do you want to do?' I said. I was annoyed with myself for letting him do all the deciding, but he'd made me feel it was my fault about not getting the money.

'I'm digging a hole.'

'What for? Why not make a fort?'

'Because if you dig a really deep hole, everybody comes over to see what you're doing. It's good.'

Sounded a bit pointless to me, but I stood back to back with him and we starting digging. It was true about people coming to look. We got down about a couple of feet and the little kids next to us stopped sticking flags and shells on their bucket-shaped sand-castles and came over. We dug out a couple more inches and Sniff arrived. He must have got fed up with running off with the cricket ball – or maybe the cricketers gave up, or something. Anyway, here he was, in the hole, growling and scraping away and kicking up a blinding, choking sandstorm.

'Get him OUT!' yelled Jason, and the little kids screamed with laughter and jumped back. I climbed

60

out of the hole, went a little way off and started to scrape in the sand, doggy-style, to try to get him interested in making a hole of his own, away from ours. He sort of got the idea. He came dashing out, lay down flat in front of me, panting and flicking his head from side to side to watch the sand rise and fall. Then he suddenly scrambled up and charged off in a big circle. Some people he passed were lying back in deckchairs, some were spread out on towels with suntan oil all over them. As he galloped through, he looked like a speedboat throwing up spray behind it, and everybody he passed suddenly yelled 'OY!' and stood up. The ones who were covered in suntan oil stood up looking like the Creatures from the Tomb of the Pharaohs. There was this circle of screaming people, some a bit sandier than others, popping up one by one among the red, white and blue stripes of the windbreaks and deckchairs. Just to finish off his trick, Sniff went flying in among the bucket-shaped sandheaps of the kids next to us and squashed all but one of them flat.

'Sniff!' I yelled. And he lay down on the last one.

Jason was keen on the idea of getting people to watch you, but I don't suppose that having about thirty of them gathered round shouting and threatening was quite what he had in mind. The kids whose sandcastles had been squashed were pretty bad, yelling at their mum and dad to get us and do us over, and even worse, there was this big bloke who kept opening his salad sandwich to show how full of sand it was. So we hopped it.

We headed for the water, mainly because it was a fair way away from the sunbathing bit and still too cold to swim unless you were trying to prove how hard you were. As it turned out, nobody chased us, not even the big bloke with the sandwich, and soon we were splashing through the warm, shallow pools down by the edge of the sea.

'Stupid animal!' yelled Jason, bending double to ease his stitch. Sniff, who had nipped into the sea to bite a couple waves, came over and shook himself into a blur behind him – and getting soaked made Jason even more cheesed off. He bent down and scooped up a little heap of sand, like tangled spaghetti, that had been squeezed to the surface by a lugworm, and chucked it at his head. It would have missed by miles, but Sniff jumped up and snapped it into smithereens. He whizzed round and round, looking for action, mouth open, tongue hanging down. He pounded the sand with his front feet, cocked his ears, turned his head sideways and Rrrraalphed for more.

'Don't,' I said. 'He's eating it. He'll only be sick later."

'Good,' said Jason. 'Serve him right for being so

stupid and getting us chucked off the beach.' But he buzzed the next one miles over his head so that Sniff had to go skittering after it.

'We're still *on* the beach,' I said.

'Yeah, miles away from everything,' Jason moaned. 'Bor – ing.'

'What about those rock-pools?' I said. 'Let's have a look in them.

'I'm fed up with rock-pools,' said Jason. 'I wanted to go down the arcades.'

'Maybe Dad'll take us later,' I said and started moving fast towards the pools. I was cheesed off with trailing about after him. He couldn't get interested in anything he didn't think of first, especially if he didn't have an audience. I looked over my shoulder for Sniff, but he'd got bored with waiting for someone to bung more lugworm casts for him and gone to find something smelly along the broken shells and dried popping-weed on the tide line.

I knelt down to have a look into the nearest pool and I saw the reflection of Jason about to chuck a rock in. 'Don't Jason,' I said.

'Why not?'

'Because I'm looking in here and I'll thump you if you do.'

'Look, there's a hermit crab!' Jason yelled.

'Where? Where?' I said, but he was just winding

me up. Suddenly we heard the sound of splashing feet behind us and Sniff was there with something sort of dark brownish in his mouth.

'Errr! He's got a rat! What a wally! They're poisonous!' Jason started backing off.

'Don't be so dozy,' I said, but Jason was legging it up the beach.

'You're on your own!' he called back. 'I'm off. I'm not hanging around getting covered in germs.' He was just looking for an excuse to get me worried or to get me to go home with him, but I knew the way back to the house and I wasn't going to go chasing after him. It was only about three o'clock, which left tons of the afternoon to have a really good nose about, without Jason showing off and getting on my nerves.

*

'But where've you *been*?' whispered Mum angrily. 'It's nearly seven o'clock. We were worried stiff about you.' She'd taken me upstairs to her and Dad's room to give me a good going over in private. Sal was asleep in the cot in the corner.

'I had Sniff with me,' I said. 'So I was bound to be all right, wasn't I?'

'That's not the point,' she hissed. 'We had no idea what you were up to. And you knew we were taking you and Jason out tonight to the Winter

Gardens. What did you want to run away from Jason for?'

'Is that what he said? He ran away from *us*,' I said. Some of the annoyance went out of her look but not all of it.

'Well I do think you ought to try harder not to squabble with Jason – you know he's got problems, you know how sensitive he is. Besides, *he* was back here before four o'clock. That was three hours ago. What were *you* doing for three hours?'

'Looking for hermit crabs,' I said, which was true, partly anyway. Dad came up and said we had to get going or we'd miss the show. Saved by The Birmingham Symphony Orchestra, I thought.

★

In the car, Mum and Dad sat in the front, Jason and I sat in the back. Jason had arranged two fingers of his left hand on his knee so that they went up and down with the bumps and kept making V-signs at me. That's how sensitive he was.

'What are we going to see, Dad?' I said. 'Is it The Birmingham Symphony.'

'No, that was last week,' said Dad. 'Sorry about that. They've got some comedy show on tonight.'

Things were looking up.

We were just driving along Margate front, towards the Clock Tower. It was still light, but all the illuminations were on. The signs on the amusement arcades were flicking and flashing. 'I was along here earlier,' I whispered to Jason.

'Where?' he said, not interested.

'In the arcades,' I said. His eyes popped wide open. I nodded. 'You know that rat Sniff found? It wasn't a rat, it was a purse – suede I think. Anyway, it was pretty old. Had a five pound note in it and about £3.70 in change. All the coins were sort of green.'

'What are you two up to?' called Mum. You could tell from her voice that she was pleased. She must have thought I was trying to make it up with Jason.

I carried on whispering to him. 'Pity you weren't there. I had a great time on the machines, specially that racing driver one. That was well smart.'

'You never went there,' scoffed Jason. 'They never let kids in on their own.'

'What *never*?' I said.

'Never,' he said.

'So how come *you* got in?'

He blushed. He actually blushed. He'd been telling great big porkie pies.

I told him how I'd got friendly with this family of dog-lovers who'd gone all gooey over Sniff, how I'd gone into three or four arcades with them, stayed for two and half hours, had a go on everything – *and* I had still had change for a couple of hot dogs each for me and Sniff. 'It was fantastic. You should have been there,' I said.

Jason went all quiet. Then he said, 'So where's the purse?' and I told him I'd chucked it. 'You're making it up,' he said. He didn't want to admit that Sniff or I could come up with something as impressive as peeing out of your bedroom window on to the roof next door. But when I put my hand into my pocket and dug out three 10p pieces, gone all green, what could he say?

Sniff and the Ghostbusters

When Jamie and Sam came round to play with Sal and her friend Tom, they always used to play Ghostbusters and I had to be Janine Melnitz.

Jamie was about five: he had this mop of brown hair and gappy teeth and he always wore slippers that looked like little animals. Jamie was the leader and he played Peter Venkman, Sam was the shy one; he kept smiling all the time and hit you if he wanted something. In Ghostbusters, he played Egon and Sal played either Roy or Winston, it didn't seem to matter which.

They played two Ghostbuster games. There was one where they did stuff out of Ghostbuster comics, called Comic Ghostbusters and the other was where they did scenes from the video, called Video Ghost-busters. Either way, little Tom didn't have a clue what was going on, but since he had a green smock and a runny nose – and he was a screamy little kid who ran about all over the place going *Nah* – they let him be Slimer. In Comic Ghostbusters he was a nice Slimer and they usually put him to bed and gave him cups of tea and stuff like that, and in Video Ghostbusters everybody ran away from him all the time and made him cry. Video Ghostbusters didn't usually last as long as Comic Ghostbusters, because when they were playing Video Ghostbusters, Mum or Dad would come in and tell everybody to stop being nasty to Tom.

Quite often, Jamie and Sam would bring the actual Ghostbuster video round to our house. Jamie would load the cassette, all the kids would sit about six inches from the television screen and stick their thumbs in their mouths. They'd seen the video about sixty million times, so they knew all the words and when the Ghostbusters said something they thought was really good, they would all say it at the same time. And when the Ghostbusters took out their proton blasters and pointed them, all the kids would jump up and start zapping, going *KAAHHH! KAAHHH! KKKAAHHH!*

The other bit that really got them worked up, was doing the Trap. Dad had made them a trap each, out of Kleenex boxes with black and yellow diagonal stripes painted on the lids. Each trap had a piece of string sticking out of the end, and when they got to that part in the film where the Ghostbusters caught a spook, they jerked it, dived on the floor, snapped the lid shut and yelled out, 'I got one! I got one!'

It was weird how serious they were. They dressed up for it and everybody had to wear what they called *kit*. They all put on yellow plastic macs, except Tom, who put on a green smock. Everyone except Tom had a belt and they tucked little clapped-out transistor radios into them for pretend walkie-talkies. They had Postman Pat rucksacks for proton packs and an old apple box for a storage facility. They wanted blasters, too, so I made some by cutting the blades off some old plastic swords left over from when I used to play The Three Musketeers with Thurston and Max. I tied the blasters with bits of electric cable to the handles of the backpacks and the kids were well chuffed.

They seemed to like watching and playing Ghostbusters so much that it suddenly struck me one day – maybe they'd like to have a crack at a real ghost. The question was, how to fix it for them.

I finally got the idea for it when I was walking past this shop in the High Street called 'Party Time' where you could get stuff for parties and hire costumes for fancy dress. I was looking in the window at the gorilla suits and party poppers and fairy queen outfits and all that, when I noticed that they had *Glow-in-the-dark* Masks on special offer. I managed to get one of them for 25p because it was a bit split, and set off for home laughing to myself and trying to think of the best way to make use of it.

When I reached the front gate, I knew Jamie and Sam were around because their bikes were lying on the front path and I could hear them screaming about round the back with Sal and Tom. I also knew it wouldn't be long before they piled into the sitting-room to watch the Ghostbusters video, so I nipped in through the front door and straight into the sitting-room. I climbed on a chair and took the light bulb out of the ceiling-light and put it in the sideboard drawer. Then I shoved the chair back by the wall and quickly pulled the cord to draw the curtains in the bay window behind the sofa. They came together at the top but there was something at the bottom keeping them apart and letting some light through. I threw myself on to my knees on the sofa, and jiggled the curtains round whatever was in the way until there was no light coming through at all. They were made of this heavy velvet stuff, so although it was quite sunny outside, you wouldn't have known. The only light coming in was a little bit through the door from the hall, and I knew it would be shut as soon as the kids came in, because Mum goes nuts listening

71

to Ghostbusters all the time and is always yelling for the sound to be turned down.

I slipped the mask over my head and closed the door to test the effect. Brilliant! It was really ace! When I looked in the mirror over the fireplace, I could see this green skull floating in mid-air. I moved about a bit and that looked *well* scary – and if I waggled my head about really fast, it made green streaks and circles.

The more I waggled my head about, the weirder it looked – just this streaky green horrible face, sort of grinning. I tried to stand still, but waggling your head about makes you feel a bit dizzy and wearing a mask makes your breath sound like somebody else is breathing in your ears. It was creepy. And then . . . WOW! what was that? Something had got hold of my legs, something tickly like great big spiders' legs – and OUCH! – sharp spines that pricked and tore at my jeans! I jumped back and snatched off the mask to try to get a look at what was after me. My heart was still hammering away like mad as I strained to see in the darkness . . . when I remembered the cactus in its pot in the fireplace. Phew! Still, it was nasty for a minute.

Good thing I'd managed to stop myself screaming out, though, because I could hear the little kids coming in from the garden through the back door! Quick, quick, quick! I jammed the mask back on and ducked behind the sofa, giggling like a madman. It was really hard to stop myself. I took deep breaths and everything, but it was still hard. I just about got myself under control as I heard them charging along the hall.

'*Whoo whoo whoo whoo whoo whoo.*'

'*Brrm brrm brm brrm.*'

'*Nah-nah, nah-nah, nah-nah!*'

'*Eee-eee-eee-eee-eee-eee-eee-eee.*'

There could have been ten zillion ghosts behind the sofa and they wouldn't have heard them, the racket they were making. One of them banged the sitting-room door open and I held my breath . . . but Mum called them back into the kitchen and yelled at them to keep it down a bit. They went more or less quiet and I heard the pad-pad of Jamie's little animal slippers on the hall floor. Then I heard him panting and straining as he stretched to reach the light switch and *click-click-click-click*.

'Mitheth Moore! Da lighth not on!' he yelled.

'Doesn't matter, darling!' comes Mum's voice . 'You don't need the light.'

'But it'th dark!'

'Well it'll be fine when you've put the telly on,' she called. 'Only don't forget to shut the door and keep the sound down. OK the rest of you – no more biscuits – off you go now – Shoo!'

I heard Jamie pushing the tape into the video and turning on the telly, and even where I was, and even through my mask, I could see the scary blue light and flickering shadows on the wall; but it was dead quiet, except for this sort of hiss. I held my breath as the rest of the gang came in and the floor bumped three times as they sat down in front of the telly. There was another bump as someone pushed the door to.

The quiet made the kids talk in whispers.

'It'th dark in here, i'nit?' whispered Jamie.

'*Nah!*' (That was little Tom. He meant yes.)

''Snice i'nit?' said Sal. 'I *like* da dark. Do you like da dark, Sam?'

'Mmmm,' Sam had his thumb in already. You could tell by his 'Mmmm' that he was scared stiff.

'Do you like da dark, Jamie?'

'I'm not thcared,' lisped Jamie. 'I'm a *big* boy and I got my blathter weddy.'

He sounded so nervous, it was kind of catching, I was beginning to wish someone would hurry up and turn the volume up because things were getting a bit *too* spooky.

One of the gang must have felt the same way because suddenly, the Ghostbuster music was pounding away. When it got to the bit that went 'Who ya gonna call?' all the kids yelled, 'GHOST-BUST-AHS!'

I gave them a good five minutes to get into the film

before I made my move, which I thought was really strong-minded of me, because it was dead hard sitting there without giving the game away. Then, ever so slowly, inch by inch, I started crawling towards the fireplace, which was in the darkest part of the room, so that the glow-in-the-dark effect would look really good.

It was awkward trying to see where I was heading, partly because of the dark and partly because of the small eyeholes in the mask, so I had to crawl really slowly and sort of feel my way. I reached out – slowly, carefully – until I felt the corner of the sofa. I tightened my grip on it and started to ease myself further forward when . . . *something* nudged me gently from behind the curtains.

A sort of electric shock went through me and I jumped up from behind the sofa as if I'd been shot. The curtains were bulging out all by themselves and there was this horrendous moaning sound. It turned into a blood-chilling, muffled howl, and suddenly, a THING came bursting through the curtains, a wicked looking thing with a luminous head like a mega vampire bat with dripping fangs!

I don't know who made the most noise – me, the gang when they heard and saw my skull mask glowing in the dark – or The Thing that came screaming at me and barged me backwards into the fireplace – YOW! – right on to the cactus.

The Thing charged on, knocked the video off the shelf under the telly and thumped into the door. As it crashed, the monster-face just seemed to disintegrate. It went out like a switched-off light bulb and at the same time, The Thing went . . . RRRAALLPH!

It was Sniff.

The gang went totally bananas. It was *hyperscreamy* in that room and then – SPLATT SPLATT – They got me! I felt myself drenched in something cold and sticky!

WHAM, the door flew open, Sniff flew out and Mum – then Dad – were standing in the doorway. Sam, Jamie and Sal shoved past them and ran for it, still screaming, leaving me and little Tom in the sitting room with the telly going FFFFSSSSSHHHHH! because the video was bust. Dad was flicking the light switch on and off, shouting, 'What's happened to the light? The bulb must have gone!'

Mum blundered into the darkness. 'What's going on? Why are the curtains drawn?' She yelled. She fumbled for the string and tugged. The room was suddenly flooded with sunlight and there I was, standing by the fireplace holding a Glow-in-the-dark skull mask behind my back with one hand and pulling cactus pines out of my backside with the other, dripping with milk and ribena.

I'd been slimed with the gang's elevenses.

So had the wall and the sofa. Mum didn't look too chuffed.

'I think this is my fault, darling,' said Dad. 'It's all gone wrong, I'm afraid.' He bent down and picked up something off the floor by the door.

'What are you talking about?' gasped Mum, looking at the wall, at me, at the fizzing telly, at Dad. 'What's gone wrong? What's happened? Look at this mess! And what's happened to poor little Tom? He's gone rigid!'

'I can explain, if you'll just listen to me a moment, Joanna,' said Dad. 'I'm afraid it's backfired a bit.'

'What's backfired? Will somebody please explain what the heck is going on here?'

'It was something I bought in the party shop in the High Street, darling!' he said, waving the thing he'd picked up off the floor.

'What was? Will you please talk sense!'

'A *Glow-in-the-dark* vampire mask. They were on sale. I couldn't resist buying one. I thought it would be fun for the kids being – you know – Ghostbuster freaks and everything . . . I thought it might be a laugh to . . . Well the truth is, Sniff was asleep under the seat in the window and I just slipped it on him while he was lying there. Zonked right out, he was – looked hilarious. You should have seen him . . . Yes, well, anyway . . . I meant to tell the children about it – you know – show them Sniff lying there – but when I got outside, I remembered I wanted to check the timing on the car – and I got distracted . . .'

'Well, darling, it was utterly irresponsible of you. Especially closing the curtains . . . And look at poor little Tom. His *face*!'

'But I didn't – I didn't close the curtains,' said Dad. 'The kids must have done it themselves. Ben, what do you know about this?'

'Never mind about that now,' said Mum, picking up Tom. 'You do something about the television, for goodness sake. I'll go and see and if I can round up the others, Quick! They're probably all in a state of shock somewhere!'

It didn't seem to cross their minds that *I* was in a

state of shock. I could have been permanently damaged after an experience like that but – forget it! Those cactus spines could have been poisonous, for a start. And when that milk and ribena hit me, I could have died of heart failure or something.

Anyway, there I was, *well* slimed, there was Dad, sorting out the mess on the walls and suddenly, there was Mum with all the little kids – Tom still rigid – standing there in the doorway with her hands on her hips going BENJAMIN! Somebody must have told her about the other spook.

*

Mum made me put the mask on and take it off about a trillion times for Tom, going, 'Look, Tom, it's me – Ben – not a ghostie or anything like that. See?' Finally he cracked me on the kneecap with his mug and burst into tears – so that was something. What a relief!

Tom's Mum, Bunty, came round, and Mum went and told her about me and Dad frightening all the little kids and making Tom go rigid and everything – which Dad and I thought was a bit unnecessary.

Bunty said it was typical, but that we weren't entirely to blame. It was Commercialism as well, according to her – overdosing little children on Ghostbusters and all that. Bunty thought that Tom had been temporarily damaged, but that with a lot of love and the right sort of food, the scars would heal. There was no mention of the temporary damage little Tom had caused my kneecap with his mug, but Bunty was happy because she said Tom had been able to release his pent-up feelings in a useful way.

I was sitting at the kitchen table having to listen to all this stuff, when I felt a little fist whack me in the back. It was Sam. Jamie, Tom and Sal were standing behind him in their Ghostbuster kit.

'What's he want?' I asked Jamie, who always knew what Sam was trying to say when he hit you.

Jamie held up the Glow-in-the-dark skull mask and all the kids yelled,

'BENJANNING! DO IT AGAIN!!!'

'Bags I get to wear the vampire mask!' yelled Dad, jumping up, with a big grin on his face.

'Oh, he's just a big kid!' said Mum, apologizing to Bunty for Dad. 'At least *that* means things are back to normal – except – oh, dear! Poor old Sniff. We've forgotten about him. He must have had a terrible shock! That was really cruel, darling, putting that thing on his face and . . .' •

'Oh, I should think he'll be fine in a few days,' said Bunty, blowing gently on her lemon tea. 'You needn't worry.'

Mum gave a little whistle to call him, just to reassure herself that the Poor Old Boy's head was still together. He came rushing in with a mouthful of knickers and pressed them into her lap.

'Ah, look,' said Mum, all gooey. 'He's brought me something out of the laundry basket to show me he's OK. Isn't that cute?' She turned to me, 'Now why don't you ever do nice things like that, Ben?'

Sometimes I worry about Mum.

Sniff, the Lilo Champion

It seemed a good idea at the time, all of us piling out of the car, taking our clothes off and jumping into the water. After all, it was a boiling hot day and Dad thought of it, not me.

We were on what Dad called 'a sentimental journey' which seemed to mean driving around loads of country lanes getting lost. He wanted to show us this farm where he worked in the summer holidays when he was a boy, but since he'd never been there by car and could only remember that the place was about six or seven miles from Wellingford station, quite near a pub with twisty chimneys, we had trouble finding it. He couldn't remember the name of the farm or even the name of the people who owned it.

'I used to call them Uncle Harry and Aunty

Nance,' Dad explained when Mum asked him for the fiftieth time why he didn't stop at a village phone box and look them up in the phone book. 'They weren't really my uncle and aunt – just old friends of my folks, and since my folks are touring Turkey at the moment, I can hardly phone *them* either, can I? Anyway, don't panic . . . this looks familiar.'

We'd heard that one before, a few times that afternoon, but at least there were signs that we were stopping. We'd come to this big sort of pond by an old stone bridge. Dad pulled off the road on to a patch of grass by the water's edge.

As soon as the engine died, Sniff and Sal woke up and started doing all the things they do when they're hot and cheesed off with being in the car – thrashing about, whining, banging against the windows, hitting me and slobbering down my neck.

'Time for a breather, I think,' said Mum.

By the time Sal had been unstrapped from her seat in the back, Sniff had bombed off into the rushes. Although he was out of sight, you could work out exactly which way he was going by the ducks and coots that suddenly shot up in the air and crashed into the water like somebody chucking bricks. Except bricks don't honk and flap across the surface of the water the way those birds did.

Sal thought it was a good laugh and tried to get into the water, so Dad had to grab her and try to explain above the sound of her screaming and shouting that this water was very wet and dangerous except for wack wacks. Mum went all tense about Sniff worrying the wildlife, and she whistled and called and worked herself up to have a real go at him when he came back. You could tell, it was going to be one of *those* outings.

When Sniff finally did come back, waving his long red tongue, he was covered in muck and smelled like a manure heap. Once she'd had a whiff of him, Mum didn't seem so keen to tick him off. I reckon Sniff had used up his last remaining brain-cells, working out how to get back to us from the rushes – because when Mum shouted stuff like 'Down boy!' 'Stay!' and 'Keep away from me!', he got really friendly and tried to jump into her arms. And when she'd pushed him away a few times, he decided to show Dad and me how glad he was to see us too.

In the end, we all agreed with Dad that – what with everybody being so hot and fed up and spattered with green mud mixed with duck-poo – it would be a jolly good idea for us all to get in the water together and have a nice cool bath. It didn't matter that we hadn't brought costumes, he told us, because he recognized this place as Noah's Mill and nobody ever came there, because it was miles off the beaten track and, when he was a boy staying with Uncle Harry and Aunty Nance, he and his friend Arnie used to swim there every evening after the haymaking. They used to ride over on their bikes – and they never bothered with sissy stuff like swimming trunks.

'Me goin in da wawwa. Me goin wimmin!' shouted Sal. She ripped off her plastic nappy-holder and chucked it at Sniff who caught it and shook the life out of it.

'All right, all right, you can go in the water if Mummy and Daddy come too,' Dad explained. 'But I think you ought to take your socks and dress off as well as your nappy.'

Mum helped Sal out of her clothes while Dad and I got undressed and Dad tried to work out exactly which way Uncle Harry's farm was. 'It must be up there,' he said, squinting now that he'd taken his gogs off. He pointed up the narrow lane to where it forked to the left by the big trees. 'Or it might just be a bit further down the other way . . . I can't quite get my bearings. We'll have a look, later, once we've had a dip and cleaned Sniff up a bit.'

Mum wasn't sure it wouldn't be better to leave our underwear on, just in case a car came, but Dad said not to bother. 'We'll only get it wet and we haven't got anything dry to change into. Honestly, this is the back of beyond . . . we'll be fine. A quick dip and we can dry off in the sun and . . .' (He held up a couple of nappies that were always kept in the car for Sal 'just in case') '. . . these will make pretty good little towels.'

So that was that. Sal's armbands were always kept in the back for visits to the swimming pool at the Leisure Centre and they came in handy. So did the lilo we used for camping which was always kept in the compartment with the spare wheel. 'You blow up Sal's armbands, Ben,' Dad said, 'and I'll make a start on the lilo.'

A couple of minutes later, we were all in the middle of the pond having a great time, Mum steering Sal about, Sal kicking and shrieking and Dad and me ducking each other and fighting to stay on the lilo . . . all of us except Sniff. He stood on the bank, still wet and stinking but refusing to come in. When we called, he just barked. When we went towards him, he backed off.

'Best thing would be to ignore him,' Dad suggested. 'Let's all swim over to the bridge. If I remember rightly, the water's quite deep just this side of it and − See the tunnel under it where the stream feeds through? − you can crawl right through it to the other side. *And* you can jump off the top of the bridge into the water.' He waved his arm to show how you could scramble up the bank and work your way across to get above the tunnel.

'Can you bring Sal?' Dad called to Mum. She nodded, turned over on her back and started kick-swimming and pulling Sal along, while Dad and I tried to shove the lilo.

'Wow! Hard going here!' I puffed. The nearer you got to the tunnel, the stronger the current became, fed by the stream that flowed from the other side. It was a great laugh and the nearer you got, the more spooky your voices sounded.

'In the old days,' puffed Dad when we were close enough to shove the lilo ahead of us into the tunnel, 'this must have been a bridge from the lane to the actual mill. Pity it's all been demolished but if you go through to the other side, you can still see the remains of the old water-wheel, if I remember rightly.'

The tunnel was cool and dark and slippery with moss, and the stream rushed through it at a heck of a speed. It was quite wide and there was room even for Dad to stand up if he ducked his head. It was great just to kneel in the stream for a bit and feel the water charging against your chest. Then, as your eyes got used to the gloom, you could make out a brick ledge that ran all the way along the side and was wide enough to sit on.

By now, Mum and Sal had made it across the pond, and while Dad pulled them into the tunnel and sat them on the ledge – and Sal was trying the echo with a scream that nearly drilled a hole through your ears – I dragged the lilo right through the tunnel into daylight on the other side. I didn't hang about to admire the remains of the water-wheel, because I had a brilliant idea. I turned round, stood the lilo up on end and belly-flopped with it into the stream. Brill! The current really took hold where the stream narrowed, whizzed me under through the tunnel past Dad, Mum and Sal and out of the other side like a cork out of a champagne bottle, till I finished up spinning round and round in the middle of the pond. It didn't half make you giddy and it was the best fun I'd had for ages.

'I'll have to try that!' yelled Dad as I struggled back against the current.

We had an ace time, Mum and Dad and me taking turns to give Sal water-chuters on the lilo through the tunnel, and when we'd all had a few goes at that, I suddenly got this idea for something *really* good. I swam across the pond to the side facing where the car was parked, scrambled up the steep bank, got on the bridge itself, even though it was overgrown with weeds and bushes and stuff, and worked my way along it until I was right in the middle, looking down at the water and the entrance to the tunnel underneath. I called down to Dad, 'Dad, are you right up the far end yet?'

His voice came booming out, mixed with Sal's and Mum's: 'Yes!'

'And have you got the lilo?'

'Yes!'

'Well, don't get on it. Just let it go with the current. Ready, steady . . .'

'Letting go . . . NOW!' boomed Dad.

I crouched down, staring at the water below, where it turned white as it rushed out of the tunnel into the pond, held my breath and waited until . . . Zoom! . . . out shot the lilo. I pushed off the bridge as hard as I could in a racing dive, and landed smack on top of the lilo which went skittering away over the surface of the pond at amazing speed. *Well* hairy!

Sniff thought so, too, because he went absolutely wild, dashing up and over the grass patch by the water's edge, barking like crazy. He still wouldn't get in the water, but when he saw Dad clambering up on to the wall of the bridge, waving and whistling, he went haring round to join him. In seconds, he was on the wall beside Dad, yapping down at me as I kicked and steered the lilo into the tunnel.

'Phwahh!' said Dad, 'What a stinker! I wish you'd get downwind, boy! What *have* you been rolling in?' Then he called down to me. 'See if you can hold the lilo just underneath us, Ben, I think he's interested in that. If he sees me pretending to dive for it, we might get him in the water and get some of this muck off him.'

'Just chuck him in,' I panted.

'No! Me tuck him in!' Sal squealed from her place on the ledge of the tunnel beside Mum.

'Wouldn't touch him with a bargepole,' laughed Dad. 'Now hold the lilo steady. That's it . . . a bit

89

closer, bit more this way, this way . . . Oh, my giddy aunt! Watch out the way, Ben!'

That was all the warning I got, and the splash he made practically drowned me.

'What d'you want to go and jump for, Dad? You've made me let go the lilo!' I spluttered.

'Car coming!' he said. 'Quick! Duck into the tunnel.'

We were so busy scrambling into the darkness to hide our bare bodies that it wasn't until we were sitting on the ledge and peeping out across the pond with Mum and Sal that we saw the lilo, going round and round in the current in the middle – and standing on it, a bit wobbly but even so, up on all four legs – was Sniff.

The car that Dad had seen from the bridge seemed to be taking its time going past. Oh, no! It was stopping.

'Look at Miff' yelled Sal, pointing. 'He's widing on da dido.'

'Sssshhh!' the rest of us said.

Two old blokes got out of the car and stood scratching their heads.

'Well arl be jiggered!' said the big one with the sun-burnt arms and bald head, 'Would you take a look at that now, Len!'

'Look like something orf of a shipwreck, don't he!' chuckled the dumpy one.

'You want to get ol' Esther Wassname on the telly down here to see this! Remember that dog what they had on a skateboard and the one what said *sausages*? I reckon that one 'ud do just as good!'

'Who d'you reckon he b'long to then?' said the one called Len.

'Now that's a thought,' said the other. 'Their car's 'ere. And their clothes, look. A kiddy, too, by the look of it, I hope they ain't come to no harm.'

'What you gittin at?' asked Len. 'You mean, in the water, like.'

91

'Well, it's deep under that bridge and there's heck of a current sometimes, where the old stream shoot through.'

'Better give a holler,' said Len. And they both yelled 'Anyone about?'

We all looked at each other. 'What do we do now?' said Dad.

'Well it's all right for you and Ben,' Mum hissed. 'But what about me? I can hardly go rushing over there completely starkers and tell them I'm all right, can I?'

'Wait a sec,' said Dad. 'Yes. They're getting in their car. Just hang on . . . I think they've decided to push off.'

We all held our breath. For once, even Sal kept quiet. Sniff was twirling gently round on the water. He likes going round and round, Sniff does. There might be a bit of a sheepdog in him somewhere.

'They're taking their time, aren't they?' whispered Mum.

'Doesn't sound to me as if they're going.'

'Oh no!' whispered Dad. 'I don't believe it.'

We all peeped out and there they were – both old gents stripped down to the nothings! Two complete nudies, one big and white as a sheet except for his sunburnt neck and arms, and the other one the same colour, but shorter and shaped like a beachball – they were wading into the water towards Sniff.

'Your eyes is better than mine,' wheezed the big one, as he reached swimming depth. 'You swim over toward the bridge, see if there's anybody what's had an accident, floating in the reeds, like. I'll rescue the poor old dog.'

'Quick! Through the tunnel!' ordered Dad and we scrambled along the ledge to the other side. Len must have been a strong swimmer, because we'd hardly got to the other end before he was peering into the gloom and calling, 'Anybody in there?'

This was too much for Sal. 'Pee-bo!' she yelled. 'There's a little kiddy in here, Harry. Quick!'

'Joanna, run for it! Up the bank there and round by the road!' whispered Dad as Harry joined Len at the other end of the tunnel. Mum didn't hang about. She was off, heading into the long grass quicker than a woofed-at wack-wack.

*

'Well I'm blowed. I'm well and truly blowed, I am,' said Harry, lifting a sunburnt arm out of the water to sweep water out of his eyes. He and Len, Dad and I were all swimming gently along, steering Sal across the pond towards Sniff on the lilo. We must have looked like a school of white dolphins pushing a pup along.

'Amazing! And I never for a moment realized! Not without my glasses on,' said Dad.

93

'Who would've thought it!' said Len.

'How long is it? – Twenty years at least, must be. You were just a boy in them days. You didn't take up farming, then?' said Harry.

'Lecturing, actually,' said Dad, blushing. 'Engineer.'

'It was you and young Arnie Chatsworth what used to come and stop with me and Nance at haymaking, wasn't it?'

'Absolutely right,' said Dad. 'I wonder how he's doing these days. And how's Nance keeping?'

'Reckon you'd better come back to the house and see for yourself,' said Harry. 'And these are your kiddies, are they?'

'Ben and Sal,' said Dad.

'And him's your dog and all?' Harry nodded towards Sniff who was still happily spinning on the lilo a little way off.

'Dat my dog,' said Sal. 'He called Miff.'

'Niff! D'you hear that, Len? Niff, they call him. He do and all. Cor, blimey, what's he rolled in?'

'It's Sniff,' I said, but nobody heard me because Harry was asking Dad where his missus was.

'I'm over here!' called Mum, stepping out from behind the open front door of the car. She'd managed to get back and get her clothes on. 'I'm the missus.'

'Oh, you're there, are you?' said Harry. 'Well I can't think how me and Len missed you. You was there all the time, look, and we thought you was drownded.'

'Well, not exactly . . .' Mum started to explain. 'I . . .'

'Right pair of old wazzicks, old Len and me, eh? It was that dog put the wind up us, see – old Niff there. He caught our attention 'cause we thought he might be the last survivor, like. So you'll have to 'scuse us, seeing as like we ain't wearing nothing but our birthday suits.'

'Well, before you get out, I wonder if you'd be so kind as to encourage old Niff to take the plunge,' Mum called.

'Seems almost a shame, don't it?' Len called back. 'He's enjoying hisself so much and he's got such a wonderful balance. Look at his old tail going.'

It was the old tail that did it in the end. The nearer we all swam, the more his backside moved to swing his tail, and the lilo rocked more and more until – over it went and Sniff slipped into the water.

A duck in the rushes went wack-wack-wack.

'There you are,' said Dad to Sniff, who was doggy-paddling towards Mum and looking sorry for himself. 'That duck says *serve you right.*'

'Don't be rotten to him,' Mum said. 'At least he found Uncle Harry – which was more than you managed to do.'

'RRRAALPH!' said Sniff, meaning that he wanted another go on the lilo.

'You'll have to hang on a mo, boy,' said Harry. 'You'll have to wait till we'm all finished with it.'

Dad, with Sal on his shoulders, me, Len and Harry all stood in a row, up to our knees in water with only a lilo to wear between us.

'Hang on, you lot,' Mum said, rummaging in the back of the car. 'I've got just the thing for you. You can all have a nice clean nappy!'

Sniff and Miss Pennyfather's Moustache

It was Friday evening, Sniff was being really annoying. I'd given him a perfectly good cassette to chew and he just sat and looked at it. The day before he'd swallowed two torch bulbs, one of the plugs out of the end of my handlebars and a bar of soap – so it can't have been the taste that put him off.

'Come on, Sniff,' I whispered. 'Just bite it a bit.'

He obviously thought it was a trap.

'*Please*,' I crawled. 'Just chew this a teeny weeny bit and Ben will get you some Doggie Chocs.' Aha. That was better. At last, the electric shock reaction – quiver, quiver, drool, drool, RRRRAALPH, RRRRAALPH.

I held the cassette under the stream of dribble. If

he wasn't going to get his teeth into it, this was going to have to do.

'Ben! Leave the dog alone and keep the noise down. We've just got Sal off to sleep, and Dad and I are trying to remember our lines,' warned Mum from along the hall. She and Dad were in their room rehearsing their bits for some Mummers' play they were going to put on outside Sainsbury's with a load of other people like little Tom's mum, Bunty. Dad was Saint George and Mum was Father Christmas. Bunty was a mad doctor or something. The weird thing about it was that they had these costumes made of strips of newspaper that made them all look like walking haystacks. Mum said it all was traditional, like Morris Dancing, and that it went back to before theatres were invented. Where they got newspaper from hundreds of years ago, I don't know, but there you go. The whole thing was dead embarrassing but at least it was in a good cause – raising money for World Wildlife.

'RRRRAALPH!'

'Ben!' (Dad this time. He didn't give it full lung-power because Sal was sleeping in the room next to theirs.) 'Keep it down. If you two wake Sally, I'm going to murd . . . Oh . . . Sally. Oh, no! Sal, will you get back into bed at once. I know. Yes, all right, I'll give Ben a smack if you get back to bed *right* now. Yes, a hard one. No, you can't watch. Now get back in your cot and Mummy and I will tuck you in. Right. BEN!!'

Time for action – Dad was on his way. Right. Deep breath.

Stand by crew. Ready lights? Sound all set?

Firm footsteps. Bedroom doorhandle twisted angrily. Door whipped open.

Roll the camera and ACTION!

'SOBSTUFF. Scene One, Take One.'

A tall, angry man (Dad) enters the room of a strong, handsome heroic youth (Ben Moore) who is seen struggling with vicious, starving hound (Sniff Moore). The hound has clamped his cruel jaws on the youth's most treasured possession, a Pacman cassette. The youth is obviously upset by the treachery of his once-faithful pal. He struggles manfully but is clearly overpowered by the sheer strength of the Beast.

YOUTH: Look what he's done! My best game! He's ruined it!

HOUND: RRRRAALPH! RRRRAALPH, etc.,

FATHER: (*Entering, alarmed.*) Ben, will you pack it in!

SISTER: (*Entering, excited.*) Dib him a hard mack. Ben naughty. CUT! CUT!

'Didn't you hear me, Ben?' yelled Dad, 'Mum and I are trying to rehearse, and now you've woken Sally up. Will you stop winding the dog up and go downstairs and get on with your homework! Joanna!

Joanna, would you put Sal back into bed while I sort Ben and Sniff out? No, Sal. No, I'm not going to smack him. No, you can't. No . . . OK, now you've done it. Now *go to bed*! Mummy is going to put you back into bed and . . . No, I'm not cross. I'm not cross. I'm smiling. Look, I'm smiling. MMMMMMMM. Right. Night night. Nighty night. I have kissed Teddy. Yes, I have already. All right, I'll come in in a minute and kiss Teddy when I've had a word with Ben. Yes. Yes. I'll do that when you're tucked up in bed. You listen out. You'll hear me giving him a hard one. Night night.'

Mum carried Sal off to her room. Now, how was I going to get Dad to concentrate properly? I did my best. 'Look what Sniff's done, Dad,' I said, holding up the cassette.

'What?'

'Wrecked my best games cassette.'

'How?'

'Chewed it.'

'Where?'

'Well . . . drooled all over it, anyway.' I held it up between my finger and thumb. 'He's completely gummed it up. My favourite.'

'This is ages old. I haven't noticed you playing this for ages,' Dad said, wiping the dribble off on his jumper and looking at the label. He marched over to my monitor and thumped the power button with one thumb, jabbing the cassette into the slot with the other. Ten seconds later, Pacmen were chomping away all over the screen. 'What's wrong with that! Perfectly OK. No problem at all.'

'It's wobbling all over the place, Dad,' I complained. 'Look at it, it's all blurred.' I gave the monitor a bit of a shove. 'What am I going to say if Thurston sees this? It's rubbish. Can't I have a few quid for a new cassette? Only a few quid. There's this really smart one – *Target Renegade* . . . and there's *Last Ninja II*, or *Odd Job Eddie* . . . You'd like that one, Dad. It's really cool. This bloke gets all these spanners and tools and stuff, right, and it's quite hard though and he has to fix this television . . .'

'Aha!' said Dad. 'I get it, I see what you're up to. You try to get Sniff to chew up a cassette you're fed up with, so that you can con me into forking out for a new one. Well, I'm not falling for it, old son. You'll have to *earn* yourself the dosh if you want to buy little luxuries. That's what I had to do when I was your age. I don't see why you shouldn't show a little old-fashioned enterprise yourself – instead of interrupting important things like rehearsals . . . and waking up babies. Which reminds me . . . Sal! Are you listening, Sal? This is Daddy giving Ben a couple of good ones . . .!'

We'd had swimming with the school that afternoon and my wet towel was lying on my bed, next to my trunks. He caught me a real crack across the backside with the end of it before I could get through the door. YOW! That was a stinger! Plus he got me on the back of my neck with the wet trunks from ten metres.

He was well chuffed with himself. I heard him saying something to Mum about not having lost the knack since he was at school; and, when I went downstairs, I had to put up with Sniff grinning at me over a little pile of Doggie Chocs that Mum had slipped him for being exploited.

*

'Why don't you go and ask Miss Pennyfather if she'd like any jobs done in the garden? I'm sure she'd appreciate a little help – and she'd enjoy a bit of company,' said Mum, the following morning, which was Saturday. I looked out of the steamy kitchen window. The sun was shining in a weak sort of Octobery way, but there was a cold wind that was knocking stiff brown leaves off the apple trees.

'I'd freeze,' I said. 'Anyway, she's such a ratty old bat. She hates kids.'

'A batty old rat?' said Mum. 'Not very nice.'

'That, too,' I said. 'She's got a moustache.'

'I don't suppose she grew it on purpose, Ben. She probably hates it as much as you do. People of your age ought to be able to rise above these trivial things and give people credit for . . . well, for getting by in spite of difficulties. She must be lonely for a start, living on her own all the time.'

'If she's got problems, she's bound to have a go at me, Mum. People like that always do.'

'I suggest you give her a chance. Look at it this way – she may need help, and you could certainly do with a bit of cash. Why don't you just see if you can't meet each other half way? She can't be that much of a bat or a rat, come to think of it, because she likes animals. She took rather a shine to Sniff when I walked him past her place the other day. Why not go and have a word with her? Take Sniff with you as a talking point. After all, she can only say no. Go on, Ben, give it a go.'

*

Miss Pennyfather's house was at the far end of Victoria Road, past all the Bed and Breakfast houses. Like them, it was a big, ugly place, uglier in a way, because it was neglected. The green paint was peeling off, and the pillars by the front door were cracked and lumps of plaster had fallen off, so that you could see the bricks underneath. There were three bells, one in the middle of the door sticking out of a lion's mouth. That had been painted over, so it obviously hadn't worked for years. There was another one in the wall next to the pillar on the right and one screwed on to the woodwork. I pushed them all and

103

then pressed the stopwatch button on my watch, just out of interest. I stood freezing on the porch, trying to stop Sniff peeing on the pillars. Fifty-five seconds. I closed one eye and held one ear close to the door. There was a sort of whistling in my ear, but nothing from the house. A minute and a half. Nothing but Sniff panting little steamy breaths. OK. I tried the knocker. Useless. The knocker was completely rusted up. It wouldn't budge. I could die of exposure out here before anybody realized I'd come to call. I tried knocking with my knuckles. All that happened was that I hurt my knuckles. That door was like a rock.

I turned round for something to hit the door with. When I bent down to pick up a stone, Sniff started bouncing up and down, thinking I was going to chuck it for him. He was barking his head off and jumping up, when the door suddenly opened.

'Don't you dare! Put that down, you hooligan!' Miss Pennyfather pointed a bony and threatening finger. 'You throw that and I shall call the police!'

I was stuck for something to say. I could see it must have looked bad. Sniff forgot the stone and threw himself at Miss Pennyfather's feet, whining and wriggling around on his back.

'That'll do, that'll do. Yes. Yes. All right. All right. Nobody's after *you*. It's that nasty vandal *with* you I'm after. I know, I know.' She bent her tall body over him and patted his chest like an expert.

I let the stone drop quietly. 'He likes you,' I said.

'Why shouldn't he?' she said, straightening up. 'Something wrong with me, is there, you cheeky little devil?'

'No.' Talking to her was like trying to ring one of her doorbells.

'Now what would a nice dog like this be doing knocking about with your sort?' she said. 'Doesn't seem right, somehow.'

I thought I'd better forget about breaking the ice with a chat and get on with it. 'Have you got any jobs want doing? I wouldn't charge you much.'

'Ah, I see. I get it. Clever little racket you've got going here. What are you, in the glazing business? Are you a glazier?'

I didn't know what to say.

'I've heard of that one before – throwing stones through people's windows and then charging them to replace the glass.'

'I was trying to knock on the door.'

'With a stone?'

'The bells don't work and I couldn't knock the knocker and I couldn't make a loud enough noise hitting the door with my hand.'

'What do you mean the bell doesn't work? Nonsense!' She pressed the one that was screwed into the wood. Nothing happened. 'Oh.'

She looked down at me. She was ever so tall and

thin for an old lady. All the old ladies I'd ever met were sort of small and tubby. None of them were this scary and angry. When she'd stopped looking at me, she turned to look at Sniff. Her face was very pale. Her skin was too tight over her bony nose and too loose round her chin. I must have been staring at the hairs on her top lip, because she suddenly covered it with her fingers. 'Bell not working, eh?' she said quietly, through her hand. 'It's no wonder I haven't had too many callers lately.' – and added, louder – 'Well, there's one job for you. Do you fix bells as well as windows?'

I said I'd have a go.

'Well come in, whoever you are,' she said. 'I've locked up all my valuables, so you're wasting your time if you think you can sneak anything past me.'

I stepped into her hall. I was quite surprised that it was so light and unsmelly. My Granny Moore has got loads of sort of dark brown pictures on her walls, but here, right up the stairs and along the long hallway, there were big bright paintings, mostly of flowers or just made up of sort of patches and splashes of red and purple and blue and yellow.

'Did you do these?' I asked, as we went through towards the kitchen at the back. I was impressed.

'What makes you say that?' she said, stopping in her tracks. 'I don't even know your name and here you are asking me all sorts of impertinent questions.'

106

'Ben Moore,' I said. And this is Sniff.' I told her our address because she was so suspicious.

'Moore, eh?' she said. 'Is it your mother who's organizing the Mummers' Play for World Wildlife? She walked by here the other day and told me about it. Is that her?'

I nodded.

Suddenly, as if she'd taken off a mask, as if a nasty skin had slipped off her and melted away, she changed completely. It was only for a second, and in that second she laughed as if she was sharing a joke with me. 'You *were* trying to knock on the door with that stone and I'm a silly old fool,' she said. She said it so fast that I didn't get what she said, I couldn't make sense of it. And before I had time to say anything, she'd changed back to her old, stiff, suspicious self. 'And what did they tell you about me, Master Moore?'

'Who?' I said.

'Did they tell you that I eat boys for breakfast, is that what they said? I do, you know. Did they tell you my name?'

'Miss Pennyfather,' I said. What was all this?

'*Mrs* Pennyfather, if you don't mind. You see! That's one thing they got wrong. I haven't always lived alone and I haven't always . . .' She made circles with her hands while she looked for the words . . . 'I used to keep things in working order. I used to bother. What I am trying to say is, I am not quite what I seem. Oh, it doesn't matter.' She covered the hairs on her upper lip again and I began to feel a bit sorry for her. Why didn't she shave, if it bothered her? Maybe she just kept it to scare people away. I was looking at this really long hair, just by the side of her mouth and she suddenly came out with, 'Do you paint, Master Moore?'

'What, walls?' Surely she wasn't going to ask me to decorate one of her huge rooms. I was looking into one as she said it. You could have put our living-room into it twice.

'No, no. Do you like to . . .' She waved her hand at the pictures in the hall. 'Do you do paintings?'

I told her I liked doing drawings, especially of firefights between aliens, and that sometimes I did graphics on my computer.

'You can paint with a computer?'

'Sort of.'

'Well that's the first time I've heard of that. I did these with a brush and a pallet knife, and your dog is eating my Rice Crispies by the look of it.'

It was true. Sniff had his great hairy feet on her kitchen table and his head in her breakfast bowl. I charged in to stop him and he caught the bowl with his feet as he pushed himself backwards. As he took cover under the table, the bowl shattered into about a zillion pieces.

Mrs Pennyfather looked at me and blinked. 'Quite a team,' she said. 'Can I expect the same treatment for my bell?' She raised her eyes towards the picture rail just by the kitchen door. There, next to one of those old-fashioned display systems with a glass front that show you that somebody's ringing from Bedroom 1, 2, 3, 4 and 5, Bathroom, Drawing Room, Tradesman's Entrance and all that kind of thing, there was a big old-fashioned doorbell mounted on a block of wood, with a big coil to work the armature that pulled the donger-thing in.

'That's it, I think. I'll have a close look at it to see if there's a break in the coil or anything. That happened to our bell once. Do you want me to clear up the bits of the bowl first?' I said.

'You concentrate on the clever stuff, young man,' she said. 'Wear the old ones out first, that's my motto. Leave the sweeping up to me.'

'I shall need a screwdriver, a torch and something to stand on. And can you show me where your fuse box is?'

'Right,' she said. 'This may take some time. But let's have a look, shall we . . .?' It took eight minutes, forty-three seconds, actually, to get all the bits together. Ho, hum. Once I was up the ladder, it wasn't difficult to see what was wrong with the door-bell. A loose connection, that was all. What was more interesting was the butler's bell-system next to it.

'Did this thing ever work?' I said. Mrs Pennyfather had finished sweeping up the bowl and was trying to tempt Sniff out from under the table with a handful of Rice Crispies. Sniff was playing safe for the moment. Mrs Pennyfather looked up at me.

'It was working last week . . . or was it the week before?'

'What, this servants' thing?'

'Oh, I thought you meant the bell. You're supposed to be fixing the bell.'

'I just have,' I said.

'But you've only been a minute. You can't have, surely . . . Just stay there!' she said and zoomed along the hall. A few seconds later, there was a DDDDRRRRRIIINGGG! that nearly knocked me off the ladder.

'So you have,' she said, coming back down the hall to where I was. 'Well, well, Master Moore . . .' She sort of leant on the ladder. She was a bit breathless after rushing up and down the hall.

'This servants' thing,' I repeated. She seemed to have gone off into a trance.

'Oh, that,' she said. Her voice went hard again. 'That hasn't worked for years, not since my husband died. It's just an old relic.' Her pale face suddenly filled with colour. 'Just a relic, young man and of no interest to me now. None in the least. Do you imagine that I intend to shower you with money in order to have you go round restoring useless, worn-out old machinery? I mean to say, what possible point could there be in fixing . . .? No, come down, Master Moore, come down.'

'It'd be a laugh,' I said. 'I wouldn't charge you for doing it. I could ask my Dad about the circuitry. Don't you think it'd be great to get it going again. Then if somebody pressed the front door bell, the little flag would go down there, where it says *Front Door* and you could have the same for the . . . (I looked at the gold lettering under one of the panels) . . . *Main Bedroom* or the *Tradesman's Entrance* . . . or whatever.'

'When I need a "laugh", as you call it, I shall let you know. Now, will you kindly get down. It occurs to me that there *is* one thing that you can do for me. I shall not be paying for the repair of the bell, of course; not after your dog has destroyed the last of my willow pattern bowls. However, I may be prepared to offer some small remuneration in return for your assistance in the garden. Come this way.

I was wondering why I bothered, as I followed her out of the back door, through a kind of greenhouse with loads of flowers in pots all over the place, and out into the garden. It looked like a park. The lawn was like a cricket pitch, and all the flower beds were full of brilliant plants and bushes, all lined up with the tall ones at the back and the short ones at the

111

front. Mrs P must have seen I was surprised, because she waved her hand from side to side in front of her. 'No, no. Not my work. I couldn't possibly, not with my hands.' I noticed for the first time that they seemed stiff and twisted. 'Arthritis, you see. Can't stand the cold. I used to do it myself, but now I have a gardener. At least, normally I do. He's away this week, so this is where you can make yourself useful. Ah! Decided to come out of hiding have you?'

Sniff had joined us on the lawn and was snooping about with his nose just above the ground making sweeps from one side to the other like a metal-detector. When he got right to the middle of the lawn, he stopped and squatted.

'Sniff!' I yelled. But it was too late.

'Well, I suppose I should count myself lucky that he didn't do that under the kitchen table. Another little job for you, I think, Master Moore. That little blot on the landscape should be transported to the compost heap which is there, next to the shed. Now, your major task is as follows. It shouldn't be too taxing for you. I'd like *those* watered thoroughly and with great care. Do you know what they are?'

I looked at the flowers she was talking about, standing in their own special bed. They were enormous, each one separately tied to a bamboo cane and standing over a metre high. They had faces the size of dinner plates with petals bursting outwards

112

like exploding asteriods, pink ones, purple, red, white and yellow.

'A bit like in your paintings,' I said. They were dead good.

'Kind of you, Master Moore. Most observant. If only there were more resemblance,' she said. 'They're chrysanthemums, rather a passion of mine. Mr Sykes has brought them on rather well. I was thinking . . .' She rubbed the back of one blue-ish hand with the other and stood sideways on to me. I could tell she was cold and that she didn't want me to look at her face. 'I was thinking that I might make them my contribution to the Fund.'

'What, the Wildlife Fund?'

'Yes. People might take a fancy to them, don't you think?' She turned to me, looking a bit worried and said to me, as though she was really interested in my opinion. 'They are rather good, aren't they? And they're actually quite expensive if you buy them from a florist . . . I mean, people might feel they are worth having, if they could get hold of them at a bit of a reduction . . . mightn't they?' She brought her hand up quickly to cover her top lip again. It was a habit she'd got.

I sort of moved a bit nearer to her to try to show that I thought it was OK about the moustache and everything and that I really liked the flowers, but she started charging away from me across the garden, shouting, 'Anyway, ask your mother. They may be some use. I don't know.' She stopped when she came to a post with a tap and a hosepipe rolled up and hung on a hook underneath. 'Do you see this?'

I said I did.

'A bit stiff for me. And I couldn't possibly hold the hose. So all you have to do is turn it on – not too fast – and spray the chrysanthemums gently. Don't knock them over, don't drown them, don't overdo the thing in any way. Just . . . just water them. They like plenty of water. You can manage that, can't you? I can trust you with a simple job like that, can't I, Master Moore?'

'My name's Ben,' I said. I just wished she would stop being nasty. She pretended not to hear. 'I'm cold,' she said. 'I can't stay out here. Keep the dog under control, please . . . I'll settle up with you when you've finished.' She left it at that, still not really looking at me, and went inside.

As soon as I started to unravel the hose, Sniff got excited. He came bouncing over and jumped up, snapping at it. 'Get off!' I said and barged him out of the way with my bum. When I'd laid the hose out so that it ran along by the chrysanthemum bed, I went back to the tap and tried to turn it on. Stiff? The thing was locked solid. I got hold of it with both hands and heaved, until I began to wonder whether I was doing it the right way. It wouldn't budge either way. I thought about going to the house and asking Mrs Pennyfather if she had a hammer or a heavy wrench or something, but I remembered how long it had taken to find the screwdriver and the ladder and stuff. So I wandered round the garden, trying to find something to move the tap with. After a while, I found a lump of wood that I could swing like a club. I took it over to the tap and lined up the end of the wood like a golfer lining up a ball, swung it back and *whacked* the tap. It did the trick all right. Something seemed to give, or snap, and when I twisted it with my hand, the tap turned – no trouble at all.

As soon as the water started to flow, the hose began

to wriggle about on the grass, and as soon as that happened, Sniff, who had been lying down watching it, jumped up and grabbed it between his teeth. I yelled at him to drop it, but it was no good. He thought he was wrestling with a boa constrictor or something and he wasn't going to let go of it till he'd bitten it to death. I tried to turn the tap off, but it just kept spinning round. It seemed to have lost its thread completely and there was no way I could get it to lock.

By now, Sniff had bitten holes right along it and water was fizzing and spluttering out everywhere, spraying out over the chrysanthemums in a fine mist. I finally managed to drag him clear, but not before both of us were soaked and shivering with cold.

Now what? I couldn't turn the tap off, the hose was wrecked and Sniff and I were going to freeze to death if we hung around. Mrs P wasn't going to cough up any dosh after what had happened – but at least the flowers were getting a good, steady soaking. I thought the best thing would be if we hopped it and said nothing. I got hold of Sniff's collar and dragged him off round the side of the house.

*

When I woke up on Sunday morning, the first thing I noticed was how bright red the sky was. I got out of bed and opened the curtains wide. Beautiful. A brilliant sunny day with no sign of clouds, and the garden looked . . .My stomach gave a sudden lurch. Everything was frosted white, everything – the grass, the apple trees, even the blue deckchair on the patio. They were thick with frost.

Without taking the time even to put on a pair of trainers, I ran downstairs, unlocked the back door, ran across the lawn in my bare feet – oo! oo! oo! oo! – it was like firewalking – grabbed a flower, pulled it up by the roots and shot back – oo! oo! oo! oo! – into the house.

I took the kitchen towel off its hook and put it on the floor by the sink so that I could stand on it and get some warmth back into my feet while I held the flower under the tap. It was a soft sort of a plant that normally had a floppy, juicy stem. Now it was stiff with powdery frost, but as soon as the powder was washed off, it turned sort of blackish and slimy. It had no strength in it, no sign of colour in the petals. It flopped over the back of my hand – dead.

The phone went. BBRRIINNGG-BBRRIINNGG! I nearly had a heart attack. I found myself dancing about the kitchen as though somebody was shooting at my feet. Even though I had to get from the kitchen to the sitting-room, I stopped it before it rung three times – because I *knew* it was her.

'Hello.'

'Master Moore,' the voice said, without asking me

117

who I was, 'I suggest you come round to my house straight away.'

'What . . . er . . . now?'

'Straight away.'

I met Sniff on the stairs as I was going up. He was coming out of Sal's room.

'Who was that, Ben?' came Mum's sleepy voice.

'Thurston,' I lied. I knew this was piling up trouble because I'd told her yesterday about Mrs Penny-father wanting to donate her chrysanthemums to the Fund. She'd said it was brilliant and they'd make a fortune. My head went all funny just trying not to think about it.

I got dressed as quickly as I could and went. Sniff came with me. He didn't wag his tail or anything. He just followed me. I think he knew where we were going.

I knew she was going to kill me, but I couldn't stop myself. I was wondering why I couldn't stop myself, and what I was going to say to Mrs Pennyfather, when I heard this loud DDRRRINNNGG sound and I suddenly realized I was standing on her porch pressing the bell I'd mended for her the day before.

When she opened the door, there was something different about Mrs P. I couldn't work out what it was. Something more springy in her walk? She certainly got to the front door pretty quickly, but that wasn't it. No, she'd changed. But as she was

118

carrying a small hammer, I couldn't get my mind calm enough to think how. At the time, all I could think was that she'd totally flipped and that at any minute she was going to smash my skull in. She didn't say anything. She just took my hand in her dry and bony hand and marched me through the hall through the kitchen, through the greenhouse-place and out into the garden – and Sniff trailed after us.

The hose was lying like a dead white snake on the sparkly white grass alongside the flower bed. And the chrysanthemums, the beautiful, expensive chrysanthemums that were going to make such a lot of money for the Wildlife Fund were standing, tied to their stakes like skinny men made of ice. Rows of ice-men, with great big ice-heads, heads as big as goldfish bowls. The water must have sprayed on them for hours before the hose froze solid. Sniff and I had murdered them and now Mrs Pennyfather was going to murder me.

Mrs Pennyfather still didn't say a word. Instead, she took hold of one of the chrysanthemums, just under the neck and suddenly, she gave it a sharp *crack*! with her hammer. There was a tinkling sound, as though she'd smashed a fragile bottle, and there, like a great red sun, like a big, wonderful sizzling firework, was a chrysanthemum flower – blooming away, just like a proper, unfrozen, ordinary, undead flower.

Mrs Pennyfather looked at me and she looked at Sniff panting quietly behind me. She stood on the frozen lawn with a hammer in her hand and she looked at us and she smiled a big, wobbly smile. 'Brilliant,' she said and a tear plopped on to her cheek. 'Brilliant. The frost has wiped out every other annual in the garden but the chrysanths were insulated by a protective coat of ice. They're perfectly preserved! Honestly, I'd never have thought of that in a million years. Thank you, boys.'

When she bent down to give Sniff a good pat on the head I suddenly realized what was different about her; she'd shaved off her moustache. When she was talking to you, she could look you straight on without getting awkward and embarrassed. She caught me staring at her clean upper lip and the ratty old bat I'd thought was going to murder me gave me another smile. I could hardly believe my luck.

'It was seeing those flowers . . . back from the dead, sort of thing,' she said. 'That was what did it. I thought – there's life in the old relic yet. Better get in better shape to face the world, talk to people, make a few chums. Do you see what I'm driving at? No? Never mind. Listen, talking of old relics, Ben,' she said – she didn't say *Master Moore* – 'Would you mind running home to ask your father for his advice about fixing those butler's bells . . . just for a laugh? Of course, I'd make it worth your while, and I think

I can find some Rice Crispies to keep your partner happy while you're gone. After all, he played a part in . . . what shall we say . . . *making* the ice or *breaking* the ice? Which do you say, Sniff, eh boy?'

'RRRRAALPHH!' said Sniff, and gave the hose one more bite, just to make sure it was dead.

Scratch and Sniff

Bruno was trying to get his dad to beat up JJ, their cat.

'Hey, Daddo,' said Bruno W. Oakley Junior, sucking the back of his hand and kicking at a molehill on his lawn with a size 13 baseball boot.

'What's up, Bubba?' said Bruno W. Oakley Senior who was reading and sunning his mega body by the fish pond in their back garden. He was wearing a Dallas Cowboy football shirt and pink bermuda shorts with purple chickens on. His deckchair bulged and creaked as he uncrossed his feet, which were so ginormously mega that his bare toes looked like five birds sitting on a fence-post. He laid *Great Unsolved Mysteries of the Universe* on the grass beside him and made a fishy face as he tried to hook something off the inside of his reading glasses with a finger like a frankfurter. He reads a lot, being a lawyer and everything.

'Would you-all give JJ a big ol' whack?'

'Now why'd ah wanna do that, boy?'

'He's just scray-atched me a *bunch*!' said Bruno.

'Where'd he scray-atch ya?'

'Back of ma hay-and,' said Bruno, shaking it towards his dad.

'Why, ah don't think you-all gonna have to call an ambulance over that little ol' tickle! He just barely drew blood is about all,' said Mr Oakley, taking a close look at it.

'But he's always doing that. He's *mean*,' said Bruno.

'So'd you be if'n you had three legs,' said Mr Oakley, reaching for his book and flicking through to find his place. 'That stands to reason. He just needs more fuss made of him than most other folks.'

'Hell, he was mean when he had *four* legs,' said Bruno. 'Ah reckon he got hisself run over deliberate, just to get us all feeling sorry for him.'

'Dern it, Bubba, you got some imagination!' smiled Mr Oakley. 'Get over here so's ah kin sit on that fat head of yours!'

'You and whose army?' yelled Bruno, running at him and pushing his shoulders to stop him getting up out of his deckchair. 'Help me, Ben, quick!'

123

For a second, he let us think we had him pinned down, all six foot eight of him, and then he boomed 'Right! That's it! By golly, you're both too dern sassy to live!' His huge body shuddered as he threw us off, jumped up and hammered his chest with his fists. When he turned to run at me, the only thing I could do was flop to the ground, laughing, roll over on to my stomach and put my hands over my head. 'C'm here, yuh little jack rabbit!' I heard him growl as he jammed four fingers under the waist-band of my jeans and hauled me off the ground.

I probably looked like somebody practising breast-stroke, but then I wiggled and bent myself in two until I managed to cling upside down to his huge right leg. Then I felt him shudder as Bruno took a flying leap and landed with WHAH HOO! on his back.

'Now ah gocha!' bawled Mr Oakley. 'You-all jumped right in ma tray-ap!'

He shook Bruno to the ground, picked him up under one arm, unpeeled me from his leg with the other, and stamped off towards the fish pond. He told us he planned to dunk both our heads.

'No! Don't! Don't!' we screamed, trying to get him to do it.

'You bet!' he chuckled.

We never made it to the pond. All of a sudden, he

let out one heck of a yelp and dumped us without warning on the lawn.

'By golly, JJ, if that don't beat the bay-and!' he called after the yowling streak of grey fur that was heading for the flower beds. 'I try to protect the critter and that's all the thanks ah git. Derned if he didn't bite my bare toe. Will ya lookit that!' He sat down heavily on the grass and looked closely at the place where JJ had nipped him.

'See! That's what ah been trying to tell you, Daddo,' puffed Bruno. 'He's one *mean* cat. *Now* what you-all gonna do about him?'

'I got a notion ol' JJ's trying to tell us somethin'. What time is it?' He looked at his watch. 'Dern it, is that right? Why that's way past barbecue time! You-all head for the kitchen and unload the refrigerator. We got some real hot Tex Mex food for me and Mommo and JJ – and burgers, frankfurters and chicken legs for you guys. Git!'

We dashed into the kitchen and there was Mrs Oakley loading stuff on to a tray from a fridge the size of a wardrobe.

'I was expecting you fellers,' she smiled. 'Now, let's see.' She started checking things off. 'We've got the burgers, the franks, the tacos, the salad, the buns, the chilli dogs, mustards, relishes, tomato sauce, mayo, pickles, salt and pepper. That should start us. I'll bring the drinks. Ice tea for me and

Daddo. If you boys want soda, we have Coke, Diet Coke, Pepsi, Cherry Cola, Doctor Pepper, Sprite, root beer . . .'

★

'. . . You sure you can't manage jest one more little somethin', Ben?' asked Mr Oakley, squinting into the smoke and jabbing with his tongs at a panful of fried onions. 'We got plenty more where this came from.'

Bruno put up his hand for another cheeseburger, heavy on the onions and easy on the mayo, but I could see Mrs Oakley through the kitchen door, squirting cream on to something made of scoops of different coloured ice-cream, sticky fruits, nuts and stuff – so I decided I'd better not.

'No thanks, I'm full,' I said.

'Why he eats like a bird, don't he?' said Mr Oakley. 'He just barely got through three burgers and a coupla hot dogs.'

'Ah sure hope you can manage a dessert, Ben,' called Bruno's mum. 'These are my specialities. You-all come in here and choose.'

I ran to the kitchen and chose the one that was laid out on a long glass dish to look like a pink and green ocean liner, with funnels made out of cylindrical chocolate wafers, with whipped cream smoke, and portholes made out of chocolate buttons, sailing in a sea of raspberry sauce. Wicked!

'Boy's, ah'm gonna leave the rest of these in the refrigerator until you're through with the barbecue stuff,' she called out to Bruno and his dad. 'Which reminds me, what happened to JJ? He usually shows when he smells hamburgers.'

'Hey, that's right!' Mr Oakley looked worried. 'Where's ol' JJ? Here, kitty kitty kitty.'

'He's just got the sulks,' said Bruno. 'He's hiding out 'cos he knows we're good and mad at him.'

'I'm not mad at him,' said Mr Oakley. 'C'mon JJ. Where are you, kitty? I got chopped frankfurters here, medium rare, just the way you like 'em.' He held out a plateful.

We all gazed round the garden. It was massive, with loads of places for a cat to hide, but wherever we looked there was no sign of JJ. We crawled about on our hands and knees, peering into clumps of flowers and sticking our heads under bushes and stuff, but it was no good.

'Let's hope he hasn't run out on to the street again,' said Mrs Oakley, looking dead worried.

'You bet!' said Mr Oakley. 'By golly, we better locate that kitty real quick.'

'Hey, Ben,' said Bruno. 'What about Sniff?'

'What about him?' I said.

'He could maybe track him down?'

'Well, I dunno,' I said, sucking a glob of peach ice-cream off one end of a chocolate funnel. I was hesitating because Sniff isn't too keen on cats. In fact, he goes absolutely nuts every time he sees one anywhere near our garden.

'Come on, Ben, he's a real neat tracker,' Bruno went on. 'Remember how he found Thurston the other side of the Rec, that day he was trying to hide out on us with a pile of Batman comic books?'

'Well, yeah . . .'

'So what are we waiting for? Let's go get him!'

'Don't be in such a hurry, Bruno,' said Mr Oakley. 'Let Ben finish his dessert.'

'Yes, that's right,' said Mrs Oakley. 'It doesn't do to go without your food. And we have cheesecake and pecan pie to follow.'

To follow? There was *more*? I said no, really, thanks, no more, honest, wow! Maybe it would be best to go straight away and fetch Sniff because . . . well in case. Wow!

'Eats like a bird,' said Mr Oakley.

*

It took about ten minutes for me and Bruno to fetch Sniff, and by the time he got to the Oakleys, he was really excited, jumping up and pulling at his lead.

'Hi feller!' called Mr Oakley from down the

garden when he saw him. 'If it ain't my favourite puppy dog! C'mon and wrastle, feller!'

He threw himself down, holding out a meaty forearm and going *RRRAHH! WUFF WUFF*. I let go of Sniff's lead and he charged Mr Oakley, barking and bouncing and shaking his head. Mr Oakley pushed his arm right into Sniff's jaws, shouted, 'Ooh you're mighty tough, ain't ya, puppy!' and then whipped him over on his back and tickled his ribs, right on his weak spot, just to the side of his breast bone. Sniff lay silent with his back leg cycling slowly, his eyes rolling, his mouth open and his tongue flopping loose.

'Honey, don't go foolin' with him,' pleaded Mrs Oakley. 'We want him to concentrate on finding JJ, don't we?'

'Aw, a little work-out won't hurt,' said Mr Oakley. 'But you're right, honey. Would you bring me JJ's little kitty-cushion out of his basket?'

Mrs Oakley hurried into the house and came out with a shiny red and purple cushion with JJ's initials embroidered on it. Bruno's dad took it from her and waved it under Sniff's nose. 'Now git serious, Sniff, boy,' he said, 'Go seek JJ!'

Quick as a flash, Sniff was on his feet, head up, ears pricked, not moving a muscle.

'He's on to something,' whispered Bruno.

'Hush, don't say anything. Let him concentrate,' said Mr Oakley.

Sniff's nostrils began to open and close. 'I wonder . . .' I began.

'Shhh!' everybody whispered.

I was going to explain that I thought maybe somebody should take hold of his lead, because once he realized JJ was around, he'd probably chase him right over the wall, right across the paddock next door, and quite likely right up into Foxley Wood.

Too late!

He was suddenly spinning, darting this way and that, scenting the air. He was on to something all right. Before anyone could stop him, he was dashing full speed . . . towards the table by the barbecue. It had a long, blue and white tablecloth that came right down to the ground.

In the middle of the table, still steaming slightly, was the large plate of barbecued frankfurters that Mr Oakley had prepared for JJ. For a second, I thought Sniff would take a flying leap and dive right on to the plate, but something really weird happened. He'd never done it before, although Sal was always trying to get him to do it – but now there he was, right there, in the middle of the Oakley's garden – begging like some yucky little poodle. It must have been the scent of the chopped medium rare frankfurters, that turned his brain to Playdough.

'Did he see something?' said Mrs Oakley. 'Did he see JJ?'

'I think he just saw JJ's supper, Mrs Oakley,' I explained. It was dead embarrassing.

Mr Oakley hurried over and put JJ's plate in front of Sniff; he couldn't stand to think of anybody being hungry.

Sniff hoovered up three chopped frankfurters, long ones, big proper Texan ones, in about three and a half seconds. He was just looking up hopefully for the same again, when JJ came out from under the table.

JJ didn't look too pleased to see his supper disappearing. He made a quick, sharp noise, like someone striking a big matchbox, took a hugh swipe with his one front paw – and Sniff was off and over the wall in about the same time it had taken him to polish off the frankfurters.

'Why JJ! There you are, kitty!' cried Mrs Oakley and snatched him up to give him a cuddle.

'Well I'll be . . . !' said Mr Oakley. 'Tricky little dickens musta snuck in under there while we were all lookin' under bushes for him!'

'Watch out, Mommo, he'll scray-atch you!' warned Bruno, but Mrs Oakley had already got him squirming with pleasure by stroking him behind his ear and under his chin at the same time.

Mr Oakley was holding out his hand to me. 'Fine work, Ben! Great little ol' puppy you have there. That was the smartest piece of cat hunting I've seen this side of the Rocky Mountains. I've heard of those English Pointers before. First time I've seen one in action though. That was really somethin'! And I reckon he was real modest to disappear like that once he'd done his job. That was somethin' special now. Mommo and ah appreciate that.'

I didn't really know what to say.

'Tell you something else I admire,' said Mr Oakley. 'Mommo, do we have a *doggybag* we can put all this barbecued stuff into? I'd kinda like to send it home to Sniff. Because I'm tellin' you, Ben, you may eat like a bird yourself – but that puppy of yours – boy, he *really* knows how to eat!'

Sniff and the Downfall of Daniel Lockspring

You had to be a complete headcase to say anything to Daniel Lockspring except 'Hi, Lockspring', because he was an animal. OK, he'd got Grade 6 for cello, Grade 5 for French horn, and always came second in Year Two exams, but that didn't stop him being the big nutter who headbutted Rishi Das's locker in.

Talking of complete headcases, the only person in the entire universe who didn't seem to have got the message about Lockspring, was the brainy pain who always came *first* in Year One exams – Thurston. He seemed to lose touch with reality completely when he got to be First Violin in the Junior Orchestra. For example, one Tuesday, about halfway through the

Summer Term, we were in the hall after school, practising for the Summer Concert. There was a short break in rehearsal while Mr Stapleton nipped off to his office to sort out some parts for the recorders. And it was that moment Thurston had to choose to shoot his mouth off about music and stuff, in his loudest know-all voice. It was all just to impress Carr, this kid on the back desk of the fiddles.

First you could hear him having a go at percussionists. According to Thurston, any moron could play percussion. This was aimed partly at Max who was on cymbals, and partly at me, on the tubular bells. It so happened that Mr Stapleton had given me the dead important responsibility of playing the loud bit at the end of Tchaikovsky's *1812 Overture*. So who was the moron? I thought I might go over and get even by practising my twiddly bits on Thurston's head, but decided against it, mainly because I'd had to borrow 40p off him for a Mars Bar and a can of Tizer. Next thing you knew Thurston was slagging off cellos, saying they sounded like a load of bees in a jam jar.

Suddenly it went dead quiet, and everybody turned round and looked at Lockspring who was sitting in the front desk of the cellos and could hear everything Thurston was gabbing about. He looked a bit egged up, but he didn't move – not at first, anyway. He just sat where he was, opened his mouth wide, sneezed, opened his mouth again and patted his hand over it – to show what a yawn he thought Thurston was.

'What about French horns?' said Hart loudly. He loved to stir.

'Flashy but limited,' said Thurston and started to rub rosin on his bowstrings. 'Not for the sensitive player.'

There was a heck of a bong as Lockspring let his cello drop on to its side. He bulldozed through the Strings to sort out Thurston, knocking over music stands left and right and sending sheet music flapping everywhere. He stood over Thurston, waving his bow about dangerously. 'Hoy, headlamps!' he yelled, 'Have you ever had one of these jammed up your nose?'

'I take it that is a rhetorical question,' said Thurston.

'Listen, sonny,' said Lockspring, aware that everybody was listening now. He didn't want to risk his place in the orchestra by sorting Thurston out on the spot, but you could tell he was finding it hard not to thump him. 'I don't like being insulted by opinionated little First Years. It brings out the violent side of my nature, right? I shall be giving you a free lesson in good manners down the Kink after final bell tomorrow. I advise you not to be late or I may have to come looking for you. Hyde will be acting as my second. I suggest you nominate a second, too, because somebody is going to have to carry the bits home. Now, we'll just make a little note of the time of our appointment, shall we?'

As he reached into his jacket pocket and took out his personal organizer, he pulled out something else with it and it rattled and clattered on the floor. 'You,' he said to Cheng, the Chinese kid with the flat-top who played the oboe. 'Pick that up. Under that chair just by you.' Cheng did as he was told and handed whatever it was back to Lockspring who pocketed it, wrote down the time of the punch-up in his Filofax, snapped it shut and, with a parting sneer at Thurston, went back to his place.

'Pretentious lout,' said Thurston, though this time he was sensible enough to make sure Lockspring couldn't hear him. The noise that had died down when Lockspring went over to threaten Thurston picked up again, and only stopped when Mr Stapleton's baton started dink-dinking on his music stand.

'He's dropped himself right in it there,' whispered Max. 'And do him good, too.' The stuff about morons had got to him.

'I doubt it,' I whispered back. 'We can't let Lockspring get away with this – he'll murder him.'

'Can't see what we're gonna do to stop the fight

now,' Max went on. 'Not now everybody knows it's on.'

'We'll have to think of something,' I said.

'Settle down, settle down,' called Mr Stapleton, his Adam's apple jumping up and down. 'Lots more to do before we finish.' He gave Wallace the recorder parts to give out, and after a bit more scraping and shuffling, he said, 'Right! We'll pick up from the Letter V where the recorders and the noise-boys get going. Watch the beat, Wilkie. Barnard, watch the beat. And ONE and TWO and YES and YES . . .'

Max and I looked at each other and grinned. We got our sticks in our hands, and stood with our feet apart ready for the off. This was the good bit that went BARRA DACKER-DACKER DAP BOOM BOOM – our favourite. Thurston was sitting with his back to us, but I knew his face would be all screwed up with worry. Every time heard BARRA DACKER-DACKER DAP BOOM BOOM, he'd be thinking of Lockspring's knuckles doing that on his skull.

*

After the rehearsal, half the kids in the orchestra went over and asked Thurston if he'd written his will. It was funny the first twenty-two times.

'I'll lend you my video of *The Karate Kid* if you

137

like,' said Max to make up for being the twenty-third.

Thurston reminded him that he already went to Karate lessons at the Civic Centre and that *The Karate Kid* was a load of junk and that he could look after himself thank you very much. He said this mostly for the benefit of Hyde, Lockspring's second, who was packing his trombone away behind us. It was meant to sound dead hard, but wasn't really very scary.

As Hyde got up and wandered towards the exit, I saw Cheng looking over towards us. 'Hang on a sec, lads,' I said. 'I want to ask Chengie something.'

I wanted to know what it was that had rolled out of Lockspring's pocket, and when he told me, it crossed my mind that the information might come in handy, though at the time, I couldn't think how.

'Antihistamine tablets,' said Cheng, touching the side of his neat little nose. 'I hope he choke on them.'

*

Wednesday morning, Thurston arrived at school with his arm in a sling.

'What you done to it?' asked Max. 'Busted something?'

'Not exactly,' said Thurston. 'But according to the doctor it's probably a condition know as 'Fiddler's

138

Elbow'. Very painful, actually. Normally only professional players get it, apparently . . .'

'To think a tree had to die to produce a head like yours, Thurston,' I said. 'Do you honestly think Lockspring's going to let you off just because you come up with a scheme like this?'

Thurston blaah-blaahed and waved his other arm about a bit, but it wasn't up to his usual standard of bluffing. You could tell his heart wasn't in it. Not surprising really, considering Lockspring was going to smash his head in.

'Look, Thurst, take it easy, will you? Me and Max have got something worked out. It's going to be OK so – just take off the sling before anybody else sees, and listen.'

'Don't tell me,' sulked Thurston, crumpling up the sling and stuffing it into his Adidas bag. 'You've talked Frank Bruno into being my second.'

'Close,' I said. 'You're having Sniff, actually.'

*

About half the Lower School was gathered at the Kink after school that day, sitting on the wall on both sides of the alley, kicking their heels and bouncing their bags up and down by the straps, or just milling about on the ground.

The Kink is this big bend where Stranger's Alley opens up by the public lavs and all the Fifth Formers go for a smoke at dinner-time. Juniors aren't allowed there except on the way to school or going home, but it's a good place for a bundle because the teachers hardly ever go down there.

Thurston was looking completely whacked out, even though it was me and Max that had been doing all the hard work and preparation, and the sweat was pouring off me because I'd had to nip home on my bike to collect Sniff.

The biggest problem had been getting Lockspring's tablets off him. There was no way any First Former was going to get near a Second Former's classroom, let alone get something out of his pocket. We did think of lowering a bit of string (with bubblegum on the end of it) out of the window at Break while Lockspring was playing cricket. Pretty long shot, that one, though.

The heat in the Hall during assembly was terrible. Two kids fainted. Max whispered, 'Why don't we let the fire alarm off?'

'What for?' I said.

He couldn't answer because Mr Jimson threatened him with a DT if he carried on talking, and I sat on the bench trying to work out how setting the fire alarm off would help us get the tablets. It was hard to concentrate with the Head droning on about behaviour at the bus stop, and I found myself looking at Cheng. It occurred to me Cheng was in

Lockspring's class and that he wasn't too fond of him. I had a word with him afterwards.

*

At the end of Period One, I was in the corridor, getting my maths book out of my locker, when Cheng came up to me.

'Any problems?' I said.

There was no way of telling from his face, but he shook his head and pushed a little plastic bottle into my hand.

'He took one pill just before assembly,' he said. 'And he left the bottle on his desk so he remember to take another pill about one o'clock. Look.' He pointed to the label that said 'One to be taken every four hours'.

'Nice one, Chengie!' I said. 'Wicked! Hang on to that until after the fight, OK?'

*

Chengie was there at the Kink after school, and so was this huge crowd of kids. They were all having a great time, chanting and whacking each other with their bags, and then suddenly, there was a really loud sarcastic cheer, as Hyde called for a gangway and led Lockspring into the middle of the alley. A big circle opened up as he shoved all the kids back. Lockspring took off his blazer and tie and handed them to Hyde.

He rolled up his sleeves and jigged up and down a couple of times, throwing punches like a boxer. The kids nearby backed off to give him more room and everyone went *'Oooooo!'*. He really was a big kid, Lockspring, and he didn't half fancy himself. He bounced about a bit more, did a few squats – and then his nose started running. He wiped it on his fist and blinked. His eyes were all red round the rims.

'Where's Wilder?' he yelled. 'Let's get on with it!'

'Forty seconds to go, actually,' called Thurston from where we were by the Gents. I was looking after his bag and blazer and stuff – everything except his glasses. Max had them. 'After all that fuss you made about putting it down in your Filofax, I thought you were a stickler for time.' He got one or two claps and cheers for that one.

'Get over here, headlamps, I'm going to teach you some manners,' snarled Lockspring.

Thurston barged into the circle, pulled by Sniff on a short bit of rope. Sniff was panting away, tugging, jumping and barking. He was really enjoying this. He stopped tugging for a second to sit down and scratch a couple of sticky-buds off his ear. A little cloud of dust came off him, like when you bang a blackboard duster on a wall.

'What did you bring *that* for, Wilder?' bawled Lockspring.

'He's my second,' said Thurston. There was a big cheer from all the First Formers.

'Listen, sonny, we're not here to muck about, you know. You're here to get seriously thumped,' said Lockspring.

'Well, you've got Hyde as your second. Sniff's mine,' said Thurston, squinting a bit without his gogs. Everyone went dead quiet, trying to work out what was going on. (*Wass he say? Wass he say?*) 'Is there some rule that says how many legs a second's allowed to have?'

That went down well with the crowd. Everyone went 'WUHAAAYYY'!

'We *are* a cheeky little brat, aren't we!' said Lockspring. He was well niggled. 'Get this stupid-looking hound out of it or it'll get my boot up its backside.' He lifted his foot to show what he meant.

'BOO!' went the crowd. 'Leave it out, Lockspring!'

'Pick on animals your own size!' somebody yelled.

Sniff's attention was on Welch who was holding out a Polo for him, so when he felt Lockspring's foot touch his tail, it really made him jump. He turned round so fast, it made Lockspring freeze. And *click* – all the noise cut out – just like that.

You could see Lockspring was worried. He knew he'd upset the crowd, even the ones who were quite looking forward to seeing him bash up Thurston. So

143

he tried to get a few laughs. He patted Thurston on the head. 'Ah, diddums,' he said. 'Do he want me to shake the doggie's hand, den?' He got one or two titters for that, so he got down on his knees and held out his huge mitt.

Sniff had turned away for a sec to look at Hart who was making stupid faces at him. Lockspring gave a sharp whistle, and Sniff jerked round, skipped across to where he was clowning about on his knees, and looked into his red eyes. Suddenly Sniff got another urge to scratch, dropped his backside and pounded away at his ear. Then he shook himself all over, a real wringer-outer, as though he'd

just come out of the sea. All over Lockspring! Brilliant!

Lockspring jumped to his feet, but there was no way he could avoid the cloud of pollen that Sniff had shaken out of his fur. I knew it was pollen and I knew exactly what *sort* of pollen it was, too, because I'd taken the trouble on the way back to school to let him have a good roll around in the long dry grass on the far side of the Rec where they never bother to cut it.

It was time to get Sniff out of harm's way. I pushed through to the front and took hold of his rope. That left Thurston all by his wimpy self, looking up at Lockspring who was hopping about with his hands over his face.

'Fump 'im, Furston!' someone yelled.

'Poor chap seems to be in some distress,' said Thurston, showing off. 'You all right, Lockspring?'

Lockspring gave a heaving, croaking cough and lunged out blindly. He missed Thurston by miles, but the crowd loved it. All the kids in the alley jumped out of the way, as though he was trying to thump *them*, laughing and cheering. And the kids sitting on the walls chucked their bags down on the heads of the kids in the alley for a laugh, or jumped down to start little mock fights of their own.

Now Lockspring really went wild, spluttering and swiping and sneezing and swearing, with Thurston dodging and skipping out of the way, and going 'HI

YAH!' like a cross between Miss Piggy and The Karate Kid. Noakes and Welch obviously thought Thurston had actually landed a couple on the big guy, because they kept yelling 'Give him another one Wilder!' Finally, Lockspring let rip with this big swinging punch that took him round so fast, he tripped himself up. Thurston was about two metres away at the time, but from his reaction you'd have thought *he'd* put him on the floor. His arms went up, and when Lockspring took both his hands from his face to try to work out what was going on, you could see his eyes and nose were streaming.

Everyone stopped shoving each other around and mucking about, and started pointing and shouting, 'He's crying! Lockspring's blubbing! It's all over! 5-4-3-2-1 KNOCK-OUT! . . . THURS-TON! THURS-TON! THURS-TON! THURS-TON!'

'Not FAIR!' screamed Lockspring, but only Max and me and Cheng heard him. And Sniff, of course. The rest of the crowd had hoisted Thurston up on their shoulders and were charging up the alley, doing a lap of honour. Even Hyde had deserted Lockspring and he'd dropped his jacket and tie on the ground. Chengie bent down and picked them up, slipping the bottle of antihistamine tablets into one of the blazer pockets as he did so. Then he passed the things to Lockspring. 'Here you are, Lockers. Bad luck.'

Lockspring snatched his clothes, told Cheng to

146

shut his stupid face, and told me and Max what he was going to do to Thurston *next time*. But it was all talk – and when he realized the crowd was coming back, he wiped his nose and eyes once more with the back of his hand and stamped off out of it.

'RRRAALPH!' said Sniff, catching us by surprise.

'I agree!' said Cheng, giving his ears a scratch. 'Nasty thing, hay fever, isn't it boy?'

'Cor,' said Max. 'You speak Doggie as well as English and Chinese, do you, Chengie?'

'Him and me unnerstan' each other very well!' said Cheng. He had to raise his voice because the crowd was bringing Thurston back.

'Thank you fans!' panted Thurston, putting his designer-gogs back on.

The crowd drifted away, shouting, 'Good one, Wilder!' and stuff like that.

'Wasn't I fantastic?' grinned Thurston, really chuffed with himself.

'Don't you *ever* learn, Thurston?' said Max.

'We better ask the real hero,' said Cheng. 'What you say, Sniff?'

'RRRAALPH!' said Sniff.

'I translate for you,' said Cheng, running his hand over his flat-top. 'He says, "You gotta be kidding"!'

Sniff Goes Missing

Part One: Dognapped

Sal reckoned Sniff had been eaten by a moo-cow. He'd been gone for three days. I was well upset but I didn't feel like going on and on talking about him disappearing. I tried to concentrate on filling a crack in the kitchen table with a mixture of toast-scrapings and a bit of quince jelly I had left on my knife, but Mum and Sal wouldn't leave the subject alone.

'Moo-cows don't eat doggies, darling,' Mum said for about the five millionth time.

'I seed him,' said Sal. 'He go nyum nyum wiv his mouf.'

'Soppy date,' said Mum, giving Sal's face a good wipe with the flannel before she lifted her down from the kitchen table where she had been sat for a clean-up after breakfast. 'Cows eat grass, not dog's.'

'Dat one on telly eated Miff,' Sal said. 'He did.'

'She's so thick, Mum,' I said. 'She's probably talking about those dancing cows on that butter advert or something.'

'NO!' Sal screamed. She came round and whacked me on the arm so hard I knocked over a cup and got butter all up my sleeve.

'Don't upset your sister, son,' said Dad, from behind his newspaper. 'And don't scream, Sal,' he said to Sal.

Sal ran across to Dad, gave his outstretched paper a double-handed whack and screamed 'NO!' even louder.

With a great *whoosh*! Dad threw the newspaper up in the air and, before the pages had flipped and floated to a stop, he dived on to the kitchen floor, turned over on his back, drummed his heels on the tiles and lay still.

Mum looked at him and shook her head. 'Now look what you've done to Daddy,' she said, shifting the high-chair out of the way so that Sal could get a closer look. 'Poor Daddy. You've upset him.'

'You've killed him,' I said, licking butter off my wrist.

'Don't say that,' Mum said. She picked up the knocked over cup and started getting all busy and nervous, mopping up the spilt tea with a slice of bread. She made squinty little signs at me with her eyes to show that it was bad for a two-and-a-half-year-old to hear things like that. I got her the sponge-cloth off the sink so that she would realize she was wiping up with a slice of bread. She threw the soggy mess on to a plate and shook her head hard, trying to get her brain together.

Sal sat on Dad's chest and pulled one of this eyes open with both hands. Dad let out a loud roar, jumped up, grabbed her by a leg and shoulder and hoisted her up into the air. He lowered her down and blew a loud raspberry right in her belly button.

'She'll be sick,' said Mum but Sal yelled 'Do dat again!' and Dad scooped her up and charged off with her into the garden.

'Dishwasher, Ben,' said Mum, absent-mindedly pushing the soggy bread off the plate into the waste bin with the side of her hand. 'It might have been the butter advert,' she muttered to herself while I loaded breakfast things into the machine. Then she said aloud, 'I wonder what put that idea about the nasty moo-cows into her head.' She turned to me. 'You haven't been teasing her, have you Ben?'

'*Me*?' I said. 'Mum, you know what a derr she is. She probably saw a tyrannosaurus zapping a Quarg on "Masters of the Universe" or something, and got it all mixed up.'

'Ben, she is not a derr,' said Mum. 'She's two-and-

150

a-half-years-old, that's all. You're entitled to get things muddled if you're her age. What's a Quarg, anyway?'

'A great, hairy alien that charges around exploding things,' I explained.

'There you are, then. What's so derr about that? Sounds exactly like Sniff,' said Mum, shaking powder into the dispenser-pod in the dishwasher.

'Yeah, but tyrannosauruses don't look anything like cows, that's what I'm saying. A tyrannosaurus hops on its hind legs, for a start.'

'OK, but little children are very imaginative. They can see similarities between things that older people can't. You see, Ben . . .' said Mum. Suddenly, *that look* had come over her face, the same kind of let's-discuss-this look I get when I ask why we can't have white bread or watch 'Neighbours' like everybody else. I couldn't face ten minutes on How Little Children Imagine Things, so I bunged a handful of table knives into the cutlery basket in the dishwasher.

'Not those, Ben! The chemicals wreck bone handles, I keep telling you that.'

Nice one. A nifty little side track. I didn't feel like a lecture, but I was in the right mood for an argument. 'I don't see the point of having a dish-washer if you can't wash knives in it,' I said.

Mum just laughed and kneed me one up the bum,

which I thought was a bit sneaky. 'All right, wise guy, she said. 'Let's not get into that one again. Let's put our great minds to trying to solve a more important question which is . . . What *has* happened to poor old Sniff? He's been gone for ages.'

I'd been feeling pretty bad about Sniff since I got up. I didn't really want to think about it, but I just knew he'd gone and he was never coming back. 'He's probably . . .' I couldn't say it.

Mum said, 'No, I should think he's fine. I'm sure he is. I just wish . . .'

'Maybe he just got a bit bored. Wanted a change for a bit,' I said.

'Something like that, I expect,' Mum said. She tried to smile but she couldn't.

'He's probably moved in with another family somewhere,' I said. 'But it's hard to believe anyone else would really *appreciate* him . . . being so smelly and dozy and clumsy and everything.'

Two big tears plopped on the floor by Mum's feet. 'Don't say that,' she said quietly.

I could see she needed cheering up. 'Don't worry, Mum,' I said. 'He'll be back. He always comes back.'

'Course he will,' she said. She dried her eyes on a tea-towel and put her arms round me. 'He's probably just . . .' she said.

'Yeah,' I said.

*

It was Thurston who suggested that Sniff had been kidnapped for scientific research – forced to smoke fags all day or to test shampoo by having it dripped into his eyes. You can always rely on Thurston to think of something cheerful when you're feeling upset. He and Max and I were sitting, later that morning, in the old chicken hutch on legs at the top end of Max's garden.

'There's a lot of that going on,' Thurston was saying through his bubblegum. 'Gognapping and Cacknapping.'

'What are you talking about?' said Max, irritably. 'What-napping?'

'Dogs and cats, you nerd,' said Thurston, flipping the gum into his cheek. 'They drive round at night in vans and grab any dogs and cats going and take them off to labs to do tests on them.' He paused to blow a bubble. Even in the gloom of the hutch you could see it swell until it was bigger than his face.

It made my stomach go all horrible to think of Sniff being caged up, being experimented on.

'How many bubblegums you got in your mouth?' Max wanted to know.

'Six,' said Thurston, taking his bubble between his

153

fingers and sucking the air out of it so that he could get it all back into his mouth. 'Why? Jealous?'

'Me and Ben have only got two,' complained Max. 'If you'd have given us one each, you'd still have had more than us.'

'Tough,' said Thurston.

'Yeah, well we always share with you, greedy pig,' I joined in.

'Oh, yeah? What about those Hershey Bars Mr Oakley brought back from Texas? You had four whole bars and you scoffed the lot of them!' said Thurston, his designer-gogs catching the little bit of light that was coming through the crack in the door.

'That's different!' I said. 'They were special.'

'Rubbish!' said Thurston. 'It wouldn't have hurt to have handed over one microscopic little chunk . . . but you scoffed the lot, so don't give me that stuff about always sharing.'

'Yeah!' said Max, changing sides.

There was only one way that a conversation like this was going to end . . . in a bundle . . . and it started as soon as I popped Thurston's next bubble with my finger and the gum went GLUCK! all over his gogs. We fell out of the hutch into the weeds, all three of us rolling over and over, struggling in and out of necklocks, getting kneed and knelt on. We ripped up handfuls of smelly plants and long grass, and stuffed them down each other's necks. I banged

154

my head on a flint, but I didn't care. Even when Max rolled on a snail and wiped it off on my cheek, I didn't mind. All morning I'd been feeling kind of foggy and miserable, but all of a sudden I felt better. I knew what to do. As we all sat panting and tucking our T-shirts back into our jeans and picking sticky-buds out of our hair, I said, 'I'm going to find Sniff. Coming?'

'Where're you going to start looking?' said Max, dabbing at the snail-stain on his shoulder with a bunch of weed.

I took a deep breath through my nostrils and spat my bubblegum as far as I could, up over the roof of the hutch. Max did the same, flicking his head to give it a bit of extra whip, and Thurston lobbed his like a grenade high into a tree because it was too big to spit far. Before it had finished pattering down through the leaves Thurston said, 'Yellow Pages.'

Max said, 'Oh yeah. Good idea. What are you on about Thurston?' Thurston didn't bother to answer. He turned and started running down the garden towards Max's back door.

★

Max's mum wouldn't let us in the house, but agreed to bring the Yellow Pages book out into the garden. She also supplied a Kit Kat and a glass of milk each. I made a mental note to mention to my mum how sensible it was to have things like Kit Kats handy for emergencies, while Max flicked through the pages. He wouldn't let Thurston do it because it was his Yellow Pages. It was dead boring waiting for him because he's such a slow reader.

'Here we go,' he said. '*Kitchens, Knitwear, Kosher Food, Label Makers, Label Printers* . . . This is it . . .*Laboratories and Testing Fac* . . . *Fackilities.*'

'Let's have a look, let's have a look,' said Thurston, trying to wrestle the book out of Max's hands.

'Pack it in, Thurston,' threatened Max. 'This is mine. You're not the only one who can read.'

'Yeah? Well at least I know how to pronounce *facilities*,' Thurston sneered.

'Will you shut up!' I said. 'Let's get on with it. Give it a rest. We've got a dog to rescue.' It just came out like that, like a line from a film or something, and suddenly we all had a feeling – I could see it in the faces of Max and Thurston – that we had a dead important mission to accomplish.

Max's finger trailed down the column of names. *ABC Laboratories*? They didn't sound very threatening. *Colour Film Services*? No. *Jarvis Concrete Testing*?

'Not unless they want to find out if he's got a concrete brain,' said Thurston.

'Shut up, Thurston, this is serious,' said Max, who had got into the spirit of the thing. 'What about this *Probe* thingy?'

156

'Let's have a look,' said Thurston and Max pushed the book in his direction. *'Probe Communicable Disease Surveillance.* That is definitely it!'

'That's the one!' I yelled. *'Surveillance!* You know what that is? That's spy satellites, bugging telephones, all that! They've kidnapped Sniff so they can give him a disease and then spy on him to see what happens! This is definitely it, lads!'

'Let's go!' whooped Max, jumping to his feet.

'Yeah yeah yeah yeah yeah yeah,' cheered Thurst, going hyper and stamping his feet up and down, like he was doing a Red Indian war dance on fast-forward.

'Hold on a bit, wait, wait, wait,' I said. 'We've got to think about this. It needs a bit of planning. Like where exactly is it and how are we going to get in there?'

'Laurel Avenue, Laurel Avenue, Laurel Avenue.' Thurston chanted, banging himself on the head with the Yellow Pages book.

'Camouflage jackets!' yelled Max and dived through the French windows and into his house. He was in such a hurry that he kicked his milk glass and sent it spinning on the paving stones. I jumped up and piggy-backed Thurston while he ran round, and managed to get him to explain where Laurel Avenue was. He stopped running and shouting when he heard Max's mother screaming at her son to get his

157

dirty shoes off the carpets. Then Max was back, panting, with three army combat-jackets, the ones with the green, brown and yellow squidged up together. One was his and the other two belonged to his dad and his grown-up brother, Alan. They wore them mostly on fishing-trips in the cold weather. Today it was pretty hot, but Max had figured it out. 'If we're going on a Rescue Mission, we're going to have to blend into the background,' he explained, helping Thurston into his dad's jacket. I put Alan's on. It smelled of fish.

Thurston and I complained about the fact that the sleeves practically dragged on the ground when we were standing up, but Max persuaded us that all we had to do was roll them up a bit. 'Now, hang on,' he said, dipping into one of his pockets and producing a tube of something.

'What's that?' I asked.

'Camouflage cream. You just rub it on your face. Like this.' He demonstrated, streaking his cheeks with a load of the muddy-looking gunk. Thurston and I did the same and then we all helped each other fill in the pink bits we'd missed.

'What about sunglasses and hats?' I suggested. Thurston reckoned he didn't need shades.

'Photochromatic, these,' he said touching the rim of his gogs. 'They go dark automatically when the sun shines.'

'Bighead,' grumbled Max, and sneaked indoors to get just two pairs of sunglasses and a selection of headgear. I chose a woollen army hat that I could roll down, Max went for a camouflage beany-hat, and Thurston decided on a balaclava.

'Cool, eh?' Thurston said. He turned and ran to the far end of the garden and lay down in the weeds by the chicken hut.

'Can you see me?' he called.

'Yeah,' said me and Max together.

'But it's only because we know you're there,' said Max. We took it in turns to go and hide in various parts of the garden to check whether we were blending into the background and, though everyone was dead easy to spot, we decided that security cameras would probably be fooled.

'Now what else have you got that might come in handy?' Thurston mused, looking round.

'Haven't got any rope, have you?' I said. 'We may have to get over a high wall.'

'In that case, we're gonna need a grappling hook an' all,' said Max looking well chuffed to have thought of it.

The first bit was easy: we just borrowed Max's mum's washing-line. Max looped it over his right shoulder and tucked his left arm through, and we hopped on our bikes and zoomed round to Thurston's big flash house.

His parents weren't in, but he said it would be OK if we helped ourselves to a few Jaffa Cakes. He opened the huge biscuit tin and peered inside. Among other goodies, there was a flat, cellophane-wrapped box that had 'Petits Fours' written on it and pictures of tasty little snacky things.

'What are those?' Max asked.

'Dunno,' said Thurston. 'Haven't seen these before.' He unwrapped the cellophane and opened the box.

'Marzipan!' I said. I could smell it straight away. We had six each – they were only small – and then went in search of the rest of the stuff we needed to rescue Sniff from the Death Lab. In Thurston's dad's office (he's an estate agent and has an office at home as well as at work) there were walkie-talkie handsets that he used when he took people to check over big factory sites and stuff like that. *And* there was also this huge bunch of keys! Great! If we had to get through any locked doors, one of these was bound to fit.

'That just leaves the grappling hook,' Max said.

'What about bending a coat hanger?' I suggested.

'No, too weak,' said Thurston. We went back into the kitchen for something else to nibble. I was just slipping a couple of marzipan things in my pocket for Sniff, thinking he'd probably be hungry, when I looked through the window and noticed that the hanging basket that was dangling outside the back door was suspended from its bracket by an S-shaped steel hook, like one of those they hang meat from in the butcher's window.

'Hey, look!' I said. 'Just what we need!' We went outside to check it out. It was quite high up and way out of reach, even for Max, who was the tallest of us.

'I'll get on your shoulders,' Thurston said to him. Max squatted down and Thurston put one leg on either side of his neck. With a bit of help from me, Max just about managed to stand up, but he was wobbling like crazy. He staggered over to where the

basket was hanging. Thurston had just reached up and grabbed it with both hands when Max's knees gave way and he fell flat on his back, leaving Thurston swinging in space for a second or two. It was only a second or two, because the bracket suddenly ripped out of the brickwork and Thurston and the basket came crashing down. All the soil, the flowers – the geraniums, the dangly stuff with the blue flowers, the moss, the ferns – everything came spraying out over the two of them as they lay on the concrete.

'Great,' I said. 'That's *really* blending into the background.'

Neither of them thought this was very funny, and they would have beaten me up if we hadn't had to get all the stuff back into the basket. There were tons of things to find room for – it was hard to think where it all went. Even after ten minutes, we could only get half the plants in, and somehow the whole arrangement looked as though someone had been practising wheelies on it.

'Oh, it'll be OK when we hang it up again,' said Thurston. 'Nobody's going to notice. Just put it by the wall for now. We'll hook it up again when we get back.'

'What about all this blue dangly stuff and this moss . . .?' I asked.

'And these ballerina-things?' said Max.

'Give me a hand to chuck them round the back of the shed, out of sight,' said Thurston.

Five minutes later, we'd got rid of the stuff there wasn't room for in the basket, and Max had lashed the hook to his washing-line to make his famous grappling iron. 'OK, guys, let's go!' he said.

'Maybe we should just try out the walkie-talkies,' I said.

'OK,' said Thurston. 'What handles are we going to use?' We chose them from the *Beano* so they'd be easy to remember. 'Right then,' Thurston went on. 'Spread out, team! Max, you go first.'

Max bent double and sprinted into the house like a soldier running for cover. I counted up to 50 before I went in, bombed up the stairs and tiptoed along the corridor to one of the big bedrooms. I stood still and stopped breathing. Nothing. I couldn't hear a thing. There was a vast built-in wardrobe all along one wall, and when I slid one of the doors aside on its silent rollers, I saw millions of skirts and frocks hanging up. I squeezed in among them and slid the door shut after me. I flicked the switch of my walkie-talkie to *receive* and stood, sweltering in my heavy jacket and woolly hat in the darkness, panting a bit with excitement, and listening so hard that I could hear the blood pounding in my ears. Suddenly Max's voice was coming over amazingly loud and clear.

'Biffo the Bear to Desperate Dan and Korky the Kat. Are you receiving me? Over.'

Before I could press the *transmit* switch, there was this mega-loud FFFSSSSHHH!

'YOW!' I yelled. 'What the heck . . .?' and as I leapt up in shock and cracked my head on a shelf, I heard another yell and crash.

I threw the door open and jumped out of the wardrobe, just in time to see Biffo the Bear himself, alias Max, leaping out of the other end. No wonder he was coming over so loud and clear, no wonder we were getting interference! He'd got in the other end of the wardrobe and hidden among Mr Wilder's suits and stuff before I'd taken cover among his wife's dresses. Without realising it, we'd been standing about 20 centimetres apart with just a thin hardboard partition between us!

We rolled about on Mr and Mrs Wilder's fluffy carpet for a little while till we'd laughed some sense back into ourselves and until Max said, 'Hey what's happened to your camouflage paint?'

My hand went up automatically to my cheek and I took a look in the mirror. Under my woolly hat, I looked as shiny and pink as a raspberry lolly.

'Must have come off in there,' I said, meaning the wardrobe. 'Yours, too. Look.' Max stood in front of the mirror and had to agree.

'Don't worry,' he said, reaching into his pocket. 'There's loads more in the tube.'

While we were muddying-up again, we remembered Thurston. 'Better call him up,' I said. 'DD to K the K,' I crooned into my handset. 'Come in K the K. Are you receiving me? Over.'

'K the flipping K here,' buzzed Thurston's angry voice. 'About blinking time! What the heck are you two idiots up to? I've been trying to raise you for ages. You must have left both sets on *transmit*. Over.'

'Sorry, K the K,' I said. 'Bit of a technical hitch. Where are you? Over.'

'I'm in the airing cupboard and it's *well* hot in here!' squeaked Thurston.

Max gave me a nod to show that he wanted to come in. 'You're coming over loud and clear, anyway, Korky. Communications-test successful. Let's regroup in the kitchen. Over.'

We regrouped, cooled down with a can of Coke each and had a few more of the marzipan things.

'What do you make the time?' I asked, and we all co-ordinated our digital watches at 12.45 precisely.

'Just like the A-Team,' grinned Max. Thurston suddenly looked as though he'd been bonged on the head with a frying-pan. Thurston went pounding upstairs again. When he got back to the kitchen, he'd got about 25 necklaces and gold chains in his fist. He lifted off Max's beany-hat and started looping necklaces over his head.

'Hey, what you doing?' Max said.

'You can be Mr T!' said Thurston. 'Pretty good, eh? I borrowed this lot from Mum's dressing-table.'

'I thought we said I was Biffo the Bear,' said Max.

'That's just your radio handle,' said Thurston.

'I s'pose you're Hannibal and he's Murdock,' moaned Max.

'Yeah, but you're the biggest,' Thurston said. Max seemed to think that was OK, and put the rest of the gold chains over his head.

I could just do with something in my belt, something a bit professional-looking,' I said. In the brick fireplace in the living-room, on a stand with a poker and a pair of tongs, there was this brass hammer. It looked *well* smart and Thurston said it would be OK for me to borrow it, so now we were all set.

'We'd better get going,' said Thurston. 'It's going to take us about fifteen minutes to cycle over to Laurel Avenue and, with a bit of luck, it should be lunch-time at the lab. That means we can . . .' He searched for a word '. . . proceed without disturbance.'

'Nice one!' said Max.

'To the Batbikes, men!' I yelled. We were off.

166

Part Two: Sniff Bounces Back

I don't know about melting into the background, but we were definitely *melting* by the time we made it to the industrial estate. It was dead hot, the camouflage jackets weighed a ton and it was a fair old way to Probe on the bikes. And that camouflage cream didn't half make your eyes sting. Or maybe it was sweat running into my eyes. Anyway, we were boiling.

There weren't all that many people about once we got to the other side of the station – but every time we went past somebody, they fell off the kerb or walked into a tree or something. They must have thought we looked dead hard in our combat gear.

Bit by bit, the streets got emptier as we rode into

the middle of the area where all the factories and warehouses are. I noticed on the hands of the Chummies Dog Biscuits factory clock that it was nearly ten past one. Dog biscuits made me think of Sniff whimpering in some cage in a laboratory somewhere and then – I had to wipe the sweat out of my eyes with the sleeve of my jacket to make sure – yes, it was Laurel Avenue. I leaned, squeezed the back brake, swung the back wheel and did a real ace skid-stop right on the corner. Thurston did the same, but Max was a bit slow braking, and skidded right into Thurston. Before he could call him what you usually call people who run over your foot, I grabbed Max by the shoulder and shook him. He turned round to have a go at me instead, but shut up when he saw me pointing. About fifty metres up the road on the left was a big sign that read *PROBE COMMUNICABLE DISEASE SURVEILLANCE*.

'There it is, guys,' I whispered. In spite of the heat, a shiver went right through me.

'Let's go! hissed Max, pressing down hard on his up-pedal. We couldn't stop him. All me and Thurston could do was ride after him.

'Don't look, don't look. Keep going, keep going,' hissed Thurston as we free-wheeled past the front of the Probe building, with its double glass doors. By just turning your eyeballs, you could see that there was a reception area with a desk and plants in tubs,

168

but nobody there. We were right about it being lunch-time. We rode past the next building which was a laundry, I think, and then turned left into the little service road beyond.

There was no sign of life at all as we leant our bikes against the factory fence. It was really hot and the only thing you could hear were grasshoppers buzzing in the dry grass nearby. The sweat was pouring off the three of us. Max heaved his coil of rope into a more comfortable position across his shoulder and twenty-five gold chains suddenly caught the sun with a flash like headlights. I twisted my belt to stop the handle of my brass hammer from banging my knee, and Thurston got his thumbs under his balaclava and flapped it a few times to give himself some air.

'Are your eyes stinging?' he asked. His gogs had gone almost completely black in the sun, but you could see him squinting and wincing under the steamy glass.

'Yeah,' I said. 'But don't rub them or you'll rub the camouflage stuff off.'

Suddenly there was the sound of a car coming along Laurel Avenue. We all flattened ourselves against the factory fence as it went by.

'Don't think he saw us,' said Max.

'Time to check the situation,' said Thurston. 'And from here on in it's K the K, DD and B the B. Right?'

'Right,' Max and I agreed, pulling out our walkie-talkies.

'I reckon we can get round behind this factory,' I said. 'And if there's an alleyway that goes along the back, it should lead round the back of the lab yard, too. What d'you think?'

'Roger, Wilco,' said Thurston.

'What?' hissed Max.

'Roger, Wilco.'

Max looked a bit mystified. 'Roger who?'

'It means *OK, message understood,* you thicko!' Thurston said.

Max thumped him one on the arm. 'I knew about the Roger bit, bighead!' he complained through clenched teeth.

'Cool it, guys,' I said. 'Max, you go first. See if you can get round the back of the lab yard and call us up.'

He strolled off down the service road, trying to look dead casual. When he reached the alleyway at the end of the factory wall, he gave us the thumbs up and scooted out of sight. Thirty seconds later, he was coming over the airwaves. 'Biffo the Bear to DD and K the K. Are you receiving me? Over.'

Thurston told him we were.

'Everything quiet here. I'm standing under this high wooden fence. Can't see a thing. Over.'

'Can you hear any barking or howling or anything, Biffo? Over,' I radioed.

'Nothing. Come and listen for yourselves. Over.'

'Roger, Wilco, Thicko, Out,' said Thurston, rubbing his thumped arm.

'Don't wind him up again,' I pleaded. 'Come on.'

Every step we took in our huge combat jackets took a mega effort and it was hard to move fast without stumbling over the drawstrings that got tangled round your feet. Even so, blundering and bumping into each other, Thurston and I staggered along the alleyway behind the factory. We paused to take a quick peek along the side passage between the factory and the lab, and when we saw that the coast was clear, we scuttled across to where Biffo the Beany-Hat was crouching underneath the wooden fence.

'Good thing I've got the grappling iron,' Max said as we joined him. 'There's no way we'd get over that fence without a rope.'

'Well go on then, clever,' said Thurston. 'Bung it up and over.'

Max ducked his head and arm out of the coil of rope. He lobbed the hooked end upwards with a nice underarm action, and, first go, the hook curled neatly over the top of the fence where there was a horizontal strut to strengthen it. He put his tongue out at Thurston, gave a little satisfied smile and tugged the rope till it was taut. Amazingly, it seemed to be holding. Gingerly, Max braced himself on the

rope, placing one foot flat against the side of the
fence, jerking once more at the rope to make sure the
hook was gripping, and lifting the other foot up so
that he could start walking up. Thurston and I put
our shoulders under his backside to give him a start.
Soon he had his head over the top.

'No sign of security cameras,' he whispered.

'What can you see?' I asked. 'Any cages?'

'No, not really,' said Max.

'Anything you could put animals in – boxes,
crates?'

'There's a couple of boxes up the other end and a
sort of shed,' Max said. His voice was shaking with
the strain of holding himself up. 'Hey, watch out!'
He half-fell, half-slid down the rope, and crashed to
the ground. 'There's a bloke! I saw him through the
window at the back.'

'Did he see you?' said Thurston.

'Dunno. He was eating a sandwich. Don't think he
was looking this way.' We all held our breath but
heard nothing. 'Here, guess what,' said Max.

'What?'

'There's a gate round the other side, right where
the shed is.'

'We'd better go round and have a look,' I
whispered. 'Leave the rope for now. If you move the
hook, it might attract attention.'

We made a commando-style run along the

alleyway, followed the fence round to the left and stopped at the gate. 'Which side of the gate's the shed?' I asked.

'That side,' Max said, pointing beyond the gate. 'Why?'

'I'm going to tap on the fence,' I said. 'If Sniff's in the shed, he'll recognize me and start barking. Max, you go down to the end and keep a look-out in case anyone's coming down the alley. Call up Korky here if you see anybody.' Max nipped off, round the corner.

'How's he going to recognize a tap?' said Thurston sarcastically. 'It could be anyone tapped.'

'Shut up, Thurston,' I said, and tapped quietly with my knuckle. Tip-tip-tip. Tip-tip-tip.

'What are you *doing*?' said Thurston.

'It's Morse code,' I said. 'S for Sniff. I've trained him to recognize it.'

'Cor,' said Max, dead impressed.

'Come off it!' said Thurston. 'He can hardly recognize his own name, let alone Morse code!'

'Sssshhh, listen! What's that?' said Max, bringing his finger up to his lips.

Nothing.

'Drugged,' I said. 'They must've injected him with something. We'll have to go in. What about trying one of the keys, Thurston?'

Thurston dug deep into one of the big square

pockets of his combat jacket and heaved out the bunch of keys we'd borrowed from his dad's office. There was this weird lock in the gate, probably just the sort they have on fences round building sites, so I reckoned one of Thurston's bunch would quite likely fit. One by one, Thurston gave them a try, but none of them would even go in all the way. It drove me crazy watching Thurston fiddling about, and every now and then I'd try to get the bunch out of his hand so that I could have a go myself – but Thurston is dead stubborn and kept elbowing me aside. Finally, one of the keys actually seemed to fit . . . it went right into the lock . . . but it wouldn't turn.

'Well pull it out and try another one,' I said. Me and Max were hopping up and down – it was *so* annoying waiting while Thurston fiddled about.

'It won't come out,' said Thurston, finally letting me have a go. I twisted with all my strength, but he was right . . . it wouldn't turn and it wouldn't come out.

'It's stuck,' I said.

'Brilliant,' said Thurston.

I suddenly remembered the brass hammer in my belt. I knew it would come in handy. One little swing and . . . DONK! the key was bent flat against the lock.

'That's done it! Now we'll never get them out. My dad's going to go spare!' hissed Thurston. I quickly dropped on one knee to see whether I could get the right angle to tap it out straight again . . .

I never did get a chance to give it another whack though, because suddenly this really scary thing happened! We didn't hear a sound, but all of a sudden the gate whipped open, an arm reached out, a hand gripped Thurston's anorak and yanked him off his feet into the yard before he had time to utter a squeak. The door slammed shut so hard, the whole fence shuddered. I dropped the hammer, and legged it as fast as I could down the alley.

*

'Now what we gonna do!' panted Max when I caught him up by the bikes. 'D'you reckon we ought to dial 999?'

'Yeah,' I said, 'But what're we going to tell them? *We were just trying to break into this place, right, and this bloke comes and grabs one of us . . .?* They'll probably say *Serves you right* and put the phone down.'

'Tell 'em about kidnapping Sniff and everything,' said Max.

'It'll take ages!' I said. 'And we don't even know where the nearest phone box is, so . . . Tell you what. Before we try anything else, maybe we ought to try raising him on the walkie-talkie.'

'That'll be a dead give-away that he had somebody with him,' said Max.

'Well at least that might stop them trying anything like . . .'

'Right,' said Max. 'If they know we're out here and we can get help, they might not – you know – do anything to him.'

'Let's give it a go,' I said. 'Desperate Dan to K the K. Are you receiving me, Korky? Come in Korky the Kat. Over.'

As soon as I snapped to *receive* we heard this voice. But it wasn't high-pitched like Thurston's. It was this man's voice, so deep it made me and Max jump.

'Hello, Desperate Dan,' it said. Oh no! He'd found out my handle. 'And good afternoon, Biffo the Bear. I am receiving you loud and clear as they say. Mighty Moorhouse of PCDS here. Korky the Kat and I have been having a little chat in the main office. I think it would be a very good idea if you were to join us, don't you? Over.'

I looked at Max to see if he thought I ought to say anything else. He looked worried but he nodded.

'Biffo the Bear to Probe Surveillance. How do we know that Korky the Kat is OK? Over.' Max put up his thumb, meaning Nice One.

There was no mistaking the shrill tones that we heard next. 'Korky the Kat here. I'm OK. Mr Moorhouse would just like . . .' There was a pause while he asked a question we couldn't hear. 'He'd like an exchange of information. Over.'

'You want to wait out here while I go in?' I asked Max. 'Then you can go for help if I get nabbed. If everything's OK, I'll send you a code-word. What do you want me to say?'

'Anything with *bubblegum* in it,' said Max.

I pushed my bike round to the front of the building and leant it against the wall by the big glass doors. I could see Thurston through the glass partition beyond the reception area. He had a can of Pepsi in his hand. I pulled open one of the double doors, crossed the outer office and knocked on the door that had *A E Moorhouse, Director* on it. A tall man, about the age of my dad but with lighter, curlier hair opened the door and peered down at me over the top of a pair of rimless glasses. 'Come in and take a seat,' he said. 'You must be Dan . . . or perhaps I should call you Desperate?'

I nodded. He'd got it in one. 'So I presume that Biffo will not be putting in an appearance until you assure him that it's safe to do so. How very wise. I must say, you chaps are not quite as daft as you look. Would you care for a cold drink? You look frightfully hot.' He didn't wait for a reply but took a Seven Up out of a fridge and held it out to me. 'I should take your mac off if I were you,' he said.

I did what he suggested, took the can from him and sat down with the anorak across my knees so that I could get at the walkie-talkie if I needed to. Funny that he was wearing a shirt and tie and not a white coat. And there was no sign of any animals, no cages, no operating tables. The office was just an ordinary office.

'Isn't there anyone else here?' I asked.

'Not at the moment, no. My partner's in Leicester today at a conference with the rest of the staff. There are normally five of us.'

'It's interesting, actually,' chipped in Thurston. 'It's all computer-work they do here. Mr Moorhouse has told me already. They keep an eye on how many people in the world get chicken pox and measles and TB and things like that.' What a crawler, I thought. He must have held out for all of five seconds before he spilled the beans about me and Max, and here he was sucking up and pretending to be dead interested in torturing animals and stuff. Still, this Moorhouse bloke didn't look like a torturer-type.

Mr Moorhouse must have guessed what I was thinking because he said, 'And no animals, not even a white rat to show. Not a mouse, not a microbe. We're only poor old statistical chaps, you see. Tapping away all day at the old computer keyboards. No syringes, I'm afraid, and I'm very sorry to have to tell you . . . no Sniff.'

'I told him what we were doing here,' said Thurston, as if I hadn't guessed. He probably told

178

him everything before his feet touched the ground. Dead hard, is Thurston. Still, I could see we'd been wrong about Probe – they weren't into animal testing at all.

'Are there *any* labs round here where they do experiments on animals?' I asked Mr Moorhouse. He shook his head and when he said he honestly believed there weren't, you could tell it was the truth. 'Excuse me,' I said, reaching into the pocket of the anorak on my lap, 'I'll just call up Max.' I brought the handset up to my mouth. 'Desperate Dan to Biffo the Bear, Come in B the B. Are receiving me? Bubblegum. I say again. Bubblegum, bubblegum, bubblegum.' I saw Thurston scratching a bit he'd missed earlier off the frame of his gogs – and Mr Moorhouse scratching his head.

*

'Good bloke, wasn't he?' said Max. It was half past two and we were outside his back gate. He'd got most of the camouflage gunk off in Mr Moorhouse's washroom, but there was a kind of dark brown frame along his hair-line and round his chin, so that his freckles were sort of lit up. Thurston and I piled our combat jackets and headgear into his arms and were glad to get rid of the sweaty, heavy things. 'Amazing he let us off, wonnit?' said Max.

'Yeah, especially when he thought you were

vandalizing his fence,' said Thurston, strapping up his saddlebag where he'd put the walkie-talkies.

'Me?' said Max.

'Yes, you. You were the one he saw clambering all over it. He was eating his sandwiches and all of a sudden, there was this mega beany-hat waving at him. He told me.'

'What about you two tapping and hammering? I s'pose that had nothing to do with you getting nabbed!'

'I thought it was terrific of him to show us his computers,' said Thurston, changing the subject. 'All those Epsons. State of the art, they are. Expensive too!'

'And all those laser printers,' said Max, not wanting to be outdone.

'*Everybody* uses laser printers, wally,' Thurston sneered.

'You're the wally,' said Max, 'getting your keys stuck in the lock.'

Thurston's squinty little eyes practically pinged out and rattled against his gogs. 'Blast! I forgot about them. They must still be in the lock!' When he said that, I suddenly remembered where I'd dropped the brass hammer but I kept quiet about it.

'Now who's the wally, Wally!' yelled Max with a laugh.

'Is that you, Max?' It was his mum's voice and she

didn't sound too chuffed. Suddenly she was leaning over the gate, shaking her long red hair and shouting. 'Where the blue, blind, blithering blazes have you been? Your dinner was on the table at one o'clock. I've been worried sick about you. And what are you doing with those jackets, you stupid boy? They're not yours to lend. And *what* have you done with my washing line?'

That was something else that had been forgotten in the relief of not being murdered at Probe. 'See you, Max,' said Thurston as he and I mounted up and pedalled off.

'Flippin' heck! Did you see her face?' I panted as we rattled up through the gears.'

'Is your mum going to do her nut about you being late for lunch?' Thurston called, coming up off the saddle to sprint alongside me as we cut past the church and into Treve Avenue.

'No. I told her I was having it with you.'

'Fair enough. And my mum's out, having her hair blued. Look, I think the best thing would be – go back to my place, get hold of a pair of pliers, cycle over to Probe, get the keys out of the lock, collect the rope and take it round to Max's . . . Have I missed anything?' asked Thurston.

'Collect the hammer,' I said.

'Don't say you left the hammer! That's antique! My dad'll go spare!' shouted Thurston.

'Well, keep your wiggy on,' I said. 'How was I to know it was antique? Anyway, we're going back for it, aren't we? And while you're moaning about some tatty hammer, you've forgotten about the most important thing of all . . .'

'What?'

'What about Sniff?'

'Oh,' said Thurston. For once he was stuck for an answer.

'Typical,' I said.

By now we'd reached the private road where Thurston lived. The road wasn't properly made up and the bikes rattled and crashed through potholes while the tyres squirted pebbles and loose stones left and right. You have watch yourself going down Thurston's road if you want to stay on your bike, so it wasn't until we were practically at his driveway that we twigged the police Panda car parked against the hedge.

'Probably something to do with Neighbourhood Watch,' said Thurston. 'My dad's the local organizer.'

In the drive in front of the house was Thurston's dad's BMW and his mum's Golf GTI convertible. So they were both in.

Thurston pressed the front door bell and it was half way through some boring tune it was programmed to play, when Mrs Wilder's blue hair appeared behind the glass squares in the top half of the door. 'There you are, dahling,' Mrs Wilder said ignoring me as she let us in. She looked as though somebody had stuck blue candy floss on her head.

'You'd better pop upstairs to your room and see if anything's been taken, Thurston,' said Mr Wilder, bustling into the entrance hall. If you put Thurston into a blue shirt, smarmed his hair down a bit more and pencilled a tufty little moustache on his upper lip, he'd be the spitting image of his dad. 'I'm afraid we've had a robbery.'

'What?' Thurston shrieked. 'They'd better not have nicked my computer. I'm half way through a program.' He thundered up the stairs. I waited at the bottom. It wasn't long before he was thundering down the stairs again. 'It's OK,' he said. 'Everything's there. Nobody's been in there. Can't we have something to eat, Mother? I'm starving.'

'Could you jest wait a maiment, dahling,' said Mrs Wilder. No wonder Thurston is such a nerd. 'Let's go into the studdeh and see what Deddy and the policeman have decided.'

The *studdeh* was Mr Wilder's office. Thurston and I sat on the cool leather sofa and picked at the buttons in the dents in it. Thurston's dad was pacing up and down angrily, and the policeman was looking at his notebook. 'So let's get this straight, shall we? This is all they took? He showed Mr Wilder the notebook.

'It's enough, isn't it? About a thousand pounds' worth. Obviously professionals, I'd say – knew exactly what they were after. Must have been watching the place. Knew we'd be out. Bypassed the alarm-system somehow, though Lord knows how. Supposed to be foolproof. Certainly cost me a packet.'

'Were you the last out, sir? I mean, you're sure you locked up.'

'Thurston was last out,' said Mrs Wilder. 'But he's terribly security-conscious. He would have locked up and put the alarm on, wouldn't you, sweetheart?'

'Of course I did,' Thurston said indignantly. 'I always do.'

'Right, then,' said the policeman patiently. 'Then let's just work from what we know, shall we? We've got this burglar. He's about eight foot tall and a bit of a nutter. He's so annoyed to find the house locked up, he goes round the back, reaches up and rips a hanging basket off the wall. He messes it about and chucks half the plants out of it, behind your shed. Right, sir? Now, he slides in somehow, without breaking any windows open or jemmying any doors, and he de-activates the alarm. Very smart, so far. He goes upstairs, nicks a load of necklaces off the good lady's dressing-table . . .'

(Oh no! That was the other thing we'd forgotten about! They were probably still round Max's neck!)

'Anyway, he's a mucky so-and-so, this nutter,' the policeman went on, giving me and Thurston a sickly smile, 'because he gets greasy brown stuff all over the good lady's dresses and all over Mr Wilder's suits where he's rummaged through the wardrobe. Now, after that, he comes downstairs, cool as you like and he has a little picnic in the kitchen. And a classy sort of greasy old nutter he turns out to be, because he steers round the Jaffa Cakes and polishes off a whole packet of . . . what do you call them, madam?'

'Petits Fours,' said Thurston's mum bitterly. 'I'd bought them specially for a rather important dinner party we're giving tonight.'

'Petits Fours, eh? Marzipan, I think you said. Enough to make you feel a bit queasy, a whole load of marzipan, I would have thought. But there you are. He's obviously not your run-of-the-mill villain. No, our nutter swallows three cans of Coca Cola, makes his way into your office, sir, and pinches your keys and three walkie-talkies. He pops back into the sitting-room and helps himself to an antique coal hammer. Bit of a collector, perhaps. Then he re-sets the alarm-system and locks up for you. Thoughtful touch, that, wouldn't you say, young Thurston?'

At the mention of his name, Thurston, whose face had gone the colour of cold porridge, started to hiccup.

'You and your chum there look like a couple of

bright boys. Have *you* got any theories about this mysterious little bit of villainy?'

'THURSTON!' exploded Mr Wilder. 'You don't mean to say that . . .'

'I'll be getting along now, sir,' said the policeman. 'I've got everything I need to know down here in my notes. If you have any further light to throw on the matter, perhaps you'd give us a buzz down at the station later on? Thanks very much, sir. I'll see myself out.' He paused just long enough to give Thurston and me another twisted smile, a nod and a wink.

★

I felt rotten as I clicked our front gate behind me. Parents are so boring! Max's mum had got her washing-line back, so what was all the fuss about? Mr and Mrs Wilder had got all their stuff back, too. You'd have thought they'd be dead chuffed to find out they hadn't had a burglar, but no. They went completely nuts! OK, it was a pity about the dinner party snacks getting eaten; and fair enough, there was a bit of camouflage cream on the clothes in the wardrobe. So the antique brass coal hammer had a few greasy finger marks on it – big deal! I could understand that he must have been a bit niggled about the keys going missing – what with people ringing up all morning to be shown round properties nobody could get into – but grounding Thurston *for a week*! And calling me a poisonous influence . . *me*? That was ridiculous. Some holiday this was turning out to be. I might end up having to play with Ashley – and worse still, Mrs Wilder was sure to phone up my mum and drop me in it!

I leant my bike against our fence and sighed. But just when I was thinking what a terrible drag everything was, there he was. Large as life and twice as smelly, charging down the path to greet me. It really was! Back from the dead and bouncing with joy to see me. Good old Sniff! Our wonderful, dozy old, long lost Sniff!

He jumped up and whined and waved his tail into a blur, and licked my face with his hot, slobbery tongue. I knelt down to get my arms round him and then gave him his favourite two-handed scratch behind the ears.

'Where have you *been*, you dippy old nutcase? We thought something terrible had happened to you.'

Sal came toddling across to us. Then she threw herself on Sniff, squeezing his head with her chubby arms. 'He's *my* dod! He gib me a big tiss.' She turned to push me away and went back to suffocating Sniff.

'Where's he been, Sal?' I asked.

'Miff dot a dirl-fwen,' she explained.

'Oh, he wasn't eaten by a moo-cow, then?'

'Yes,' said Sal, shaking her head seriously. 'He goed nyum nyum wiv his mouf – but he spitted him out after.'

I went in and asked Mum for more details. It turned out he'd spent the last two nights under sombody's hedge, rolling his eyes and howling for his lady love to come out.

'Was she on heat?' I asked.

'Oh, you know about that, do you?' Mum said. 'Well that saves me having to explain.'

'I'm surprised the people didn't do something about him if he was there making a nuisance of himself for all that time. Who were they?'

'That little cul-de-sac where they just built the new

188

bungalows. The people had just moved in. Nervous types, I suppose.'

'A bucket of water would have shifted him,' I said.

'Quite,' said Mum. 'Not too fond of water, are you boy?' Sniff looked at her with sad brown eyes. 'Just like Ben and Sal, in fact.' She tugged his ears affectionately and smiled up at me. 'Your face is particularly mucky today, Ben, dear."

'Don't fuss, Mum,' I said.

'Is your fussy old mum allowed to enquire what you've been up to? I suppose it never crossed your mind to spend some time looking for our long lost darling doggy.'

The phone began to ring. Oh, no! The Bells of Doom!

'You'd be really pleased if I told you we'd been out all day trying to find him, wouldn't you . . .?' I said quickly as she started moving to answer it.

'That would have been really nice,' she said, giving me a bit of a sideways look. 'Why?'

'In other words, you'd have been really, really chuffed with me trying to get Sniff back. Right? Really over the moon . . .?'

She'd picked up the phone but she was smiling and nodding. 'Hello? Ah, yes, Mrs Wilder, this is Ben's mum . . .'

I didn't hang about. I was off. Time to melt into the background again . . . after a quick whistle. Whatever happened, one thing was for sure – there was nothing to beat the sound of Sniff pounding up the stairs behind me.

Other great reads *from* **Red Fox**

THE SNIFF STORIES   Ian Whybrow

Things just keep happening to Ben Moore. It's dead hard avoiding disaster when you've got to keep your street cred with your mates *and* cope with a family of oddballs at the same time. There's his appalling 2½ year old sister, his scatty parents who are into healthy eating and animal rights and, worse than all of these, there's Sniff! If only Ben could just get on with his scientific experiments and his attempt at a world beating *Swampbeast* score . . . but there's no chance of that while chaos is just around the corner.

ISBN 0 09 9750406   £2.50

J.B. SUPERSLEUTH   Joan Davenport

James Bond is a small thirteen-year-old with spots and spectacles. But with a name like that, how can he help being a supersleuth?

It all started when James and 'Polly' (Paul) Perkins spotted a teacher's stolen car. After that, more and more mysteries needed solving. With the case of the Arabian prince, the Murdered Model, the Bonfire Night Murder and the Lost Umbrella, JB's reputation at Moorside Comprehensive soars.

But some of the cases aren't quite what they seem . . .

ISBN 0 09 9717808   £1.99

Other great reads ⟍ *from* **Red Fox**

Discover the exciting and hilarious books of Hazel Townson!

THE MOVING STATUE

One windy day in the middle of his paper round, Jason Riddle is blown against the town's war memorial statue.

But the statue moves its foot! Can this be true?

ISBN 0 09 973370 6 £1.99

ONE GREEN BOTTLE

Tim Evans has invented a fantasic new board game called REDUNDO. But after he leaves it at his local toy shop it disappears! Could Mr Snyder, the wily toy shop owner have stolen the game to develop it for himself? Tim and his friend Doggo decide to take drastic action and with the help of a mysterious green bottle, plan a Reign of Terror.

ISBN 0 09 956810 1 £1.50

THE SPECKLED PANIC

When Kip buys Venger's Speckled Truthpaste instead of toothpaste, funny things start happening. But they get out of control when the headmaster eats some by mistake. What terrible truths will he tell the parents on speech day?

ISBN 0 09 935490 X £1.75

THE CHOKING PERIL

In this sequel to *The Speckled Panic*, Herbie, Kip and Arthur Venger the inventor attempt to reform Grumpton's litterbugs.

ISBN 0 09 950530 4 £1.25